A Dead End

A Saints & Strangers Cozy Mystery

Book One

Keeley Bates

This is a work of fiction. Names, characters, businesses, places, events and incidents are either the products of the author's imagination or used in a fictitious manner. Any resemblance to actual persons, living or dead, or actual events is purely coincidental.

Cover Design by Cover Kicks

Special thanks to Dr. Colleen Farrell for her infinite wisdom regarding all things medical.

Chapter One

Kit Wilder did not have moves like Jagger. Quite the contrary, she fully recognized that her moves were more of the Elaine from Seinfeld variety, which was why her agent, Beatrice Coleman, said she would never be invited to appear on Dancing with the Stars no matter how many times Beatrice attempted to cattle prod the producers into submission. This disappointed Beatrice more than Katherine, as Beatrice was a fan of the show and her other clients weren't attractive or popular enough to qualify.

Kit finished her dance cardio session with a sense of relief, not because she accomplished a full hour's workout but because she did it without any witnesses. Although she could perform fight scenes with grace and precision, she had no sense of rhythm. She wasn't sure where this particular dance cardio guru came up with some of her more complex moves. It was like playing Twister while avoiding the hot flames that licked the bottom of your feet. Removing her ear buds, she vowed to get back to good, old-fashioned exercises like spinning. Why did the easy ones tend to fall out of fashion?

She grabbed her iPhone and snapped a photo of herself glistening with sweat and bearing a wide grin. Within two minutes she shared it on Instagram and then tweeted it to her fans along with a message about the number of calories burned so far today. She knew many of her followers would still be asleep in America, but there were more than a few in California who'd still be active at this hour. Her best friend, Jordan, among them.

An instructor entered the studio, surprised to see Kit. The instructor clearly didn't recognize her, not that she expected to be recognized in London. Unsurprisingly, her show had been more popular in America than anywhere else.

"Are you here for my class?" the instructor asked.

Kit tucked her iPhone into her sports bra. "No, sorry. I just didn't have enough space in my hotel room for my Tracy Anderson DVD."

The instructor gave her a quizzical look. "But there's no television in here."

Kit tapped the side of her head. "It's all up here. Like memorizing lines."

Kit took the elevator from the gym back up to her hotel room. Today was her last day on the set of the period drama and marked the last official day of her acting career, for now. The part was small, a favor owed by a London agent to Beatrice. Kit had a few lines ('More tea, Madam?' and 'Yes, Madam') and the cast was highly regarded. She'd been highly regarded until recently.

As an eighteen-year-old ingénue, Kit shot to fame as rookie detective Ellie Gold on the hit show, Fool's Gold. She graced the covers of all the major magazines and even had a famous catchphrase – 'I got your bling right here,' usually uttered while producing a set of gleaming handcuffs. She still had the T-shirt in three different colors to prove it.

Over the course of four seasons, she made one strategic error after another, earning herself the label of diva. Kit was well-acquainted with divas having been raised by one in affluent Westdale, Pennsylvania and she knew that she didn't fit the bill. Of course, in Hollywood 'diva' was code for troublemaker or as the producer had called her before showing her the door — the resident rebel rouser. Okay, so she may have made a few teeny tiny waves after complaining publicly about the treatment of crew members, refusing to wear high heels to a red carpet event, and reporting a line producer for several instances of sexual harassment. Seth, her A-list agent at the time, had tried to talk her out of each action by reciting a long list of those actors who had made similar bad choices — those actors who now languished in acting purgatory. Kit, however, thoroughly believed that her star was on the rise and that the force of gravity was no obstacle. She'd wanted to use her power for good. As a reward for her 'good' behavior, her character was killed off and she was blackballed by producers. So much for having a conscience in Hollywood.

Thanks to ballbusting Beatrice, the fairy godmother agent who rescued her after Seth's departure, Kit briefly attempted to pursue an independent film career. Even they wouldn't touch her. Blackballing aside, they deemed her box office poison because of the movies she'd filmed during previous hiatuses that had tanked. It turned out that American audiences did not want to see her in rom-coms alongside vaguely attractive comedians-turned-actors. They wanted her in uniform with appropriate cleavage, uttering her catchphrase with a thick New Jersey accent. Lesson learned. Unfortunately for her, indie producers had learned it, too.

As she undressed for the shower, swallowing the taste of regret, the sound of It's Raining Men startled her. She pulled her phone out of her bra.

"Hi Jordan." Jordan Newberg was the wardrobe designer for Fool's Gold and Kit's best friend — the one and only person she was sorry to leave behind when she left California.

"You popped up in my Twitter feed. Are you feeling unloved again? Aren't you with your mother by now?"

Kit put Jordan on speaker and continued to undress. "First of all, you know perfectly well that my mother and feeling unloved go hand-in-hand. Second of all, I'm still in London. Today's the last day."

"Then you're back to Westdale." Jordan sighed. "Have you told Mumsy about the house?"

Kit turned on the water for the shower. "Not yet. She'll figure it out when I leave Greyabbey to sleep somewhere else."

"When do classes start?"

"Two weeks. That should give me time to get started on the renovations."

"Kit Wilder doing DIY. I'd pay good money to see that."

"Pay for a plane ticket and you can have a front row seat."

"Would love to, darling, but duty calls. Besides, I'd rather have a front row seat to your reunion with Mumsy."

"Stop calling her that," Kit scoffed. "I call her Mother and you know it."

"I thought all rich people said Mumsy," he teased. "It's in the Wealthy White Person Handbook."

"Going now," Kit said and clicked off the phone. Steam had already filled the bathroom. She stepped inside and closed the shower door, determined to wash away all evidence of failure before her return to Westdale.

Kit yawned and stretched as the cab drove down Standish Street, past Liberty Square, and turned onto Tulane Street. She hadn't been back to Westdale since she left five years ago, three weeks after her father's funeral. Douglas Wilder's heart attack had been a great shock to everyone and, as his only child, Kit was desperate to escape the pain of his sudden absence.

Unsurprisingly, the town looked just the same. The square was as picturesque as ever, with shoppers strolling down Standish Street. Butter Beans, the coffee shop, still enjoyed its prominent position at the front of the square, luring everyone in Westdale with their cozy atmosphere and exotic coffees and teas. In fact, Butter Beans looked really good to Kit right now.

The cab continued down Tulane Street, past the library, and turned briefly onto Keystone Road until turning onto Thornhill Road and Kit's new home. She'd used the last of her Fool's Gold money to buy the foreclosed house. It needed work, but Kit wasn't afraid of rolling up her sleeves. She'd grown up a lot during her time in Los Angeles. She only hoped that she could hold on to that maturity now that she was back on childhood soil. Chances were slim.

The cabbie removed her luggage from the trunk and carried the bags to the door.

"I got your bags right here," he declared, standing on the front porch, the glee evident on his face.

Kit forced a smile. "You've seen the show." He wasn't the first person to abuse her catchphrase and he wouldn't be the last.

"I didn't recognize you at first," the cabbie confessed. He glanced at the unkempt house. "This is where you're living now?"

"Yes," Kit answered a touch defensively. "I'm starting college this semester. I thought it was time to focus on my education."

The cabbie nodded approvingly. "Well, Westdale College has a great reputation. You must be a smart girl."

Kit paid him and doubled the tip. No one would ever accuse her of being cheap, at least when it came to other people. "I had a little help."

Actually, she'd had a lot of help. Her mother, Heloise Winthrop Wilder, had pulled a few strings to get Kit a place in the first year class. Kit's college entrance scores weren't recent and her grades at the Shiphay School had been only slightly above average in a sea of ambitious overachievers. This was what her mother wanted, though, and Heloise Winthrop Wilder generally got what she wanted, even if she had to wait five years to get it.

Kit unlocked the front door for the first time and peered inside. Stale air filled her nostrils. Myra Beacon, the realtor had sent a plethora of photos, wanting to be certain that Kit knew what she was getting herself into. She did. Without television money or her trust fund, she needed a fixer upper and this was, quite literally, the only one in town. Her mother had agreed to pay for college but refused to reinstate

6

her trust fund. Kit was still being punished for fleeing to Los Angeles after her father's death. It didn't matter that Douglas Wilder had encouraged Kit to follow her dreams before he died. It only mattered that Kit had left Westdale to pursue a career that was, God forbid, beneath the dignity of the Winthrop Wilders. She may as well have announced that she'd launched an online sex video.

There were a few packages to the left of the front door addressed to her, along with a welcome note from Myra. Kit recognized Jordan's expressive handwriting on a medium-sized square box and smiled. She'd open it as soon as she aired out the house.

Kit set to work opening the windows and touring her new house. Most of her belongings were in a storage unit in nearby Media until she completed the renovations. Beatrice had gone above and beyond the call of duty when it came to Kit's relocation. She'd organized the moving company while Kit was in London and convinced Kit's entertainment lawyer to handle the purchase of the house on Thornhill. It was nice knowing that someone was in her corner. By the time she'd shot her last scene on Fool's Gold, she'd felt like all her butt was missing was a footprint.

Kit surveyed the living room with a critical eye. The white wooden mantelpiece was pretty and understated. The walls were a faded duck egg blue — they would need a fresh coat of paint. Her eyes dropped to the blush-colored carpet. It was hideous in its own right, but it looked even worse in a room with duck egg blue walls. Only a straight man who lived alone would conjure up this look. Too bad the carpet looked as good as new. Maybe if she ripped it up carefully, someone else would be able to use it. Kit knew that most

Westdale houses had beautiful hardwood floors underneath and she was happy to revive them. She'd spent enough time with the television crew to know how to strip and sand a floor. What she didn't know, she'd Google. She was pretty sure that was why the internet was invented.

The sound of a screeching violin interrupted her thoughts. The theme from Psycho. Reluctantly, she pulled her phone from her pocket. "Hello, Mother."

"Katherine Clementine Winthrop Wilder, how long do you expect to hide from me?" Her mother's sharp voice echoed in her ear and Kit switched to speaker mode.

"I'm not hiding," she argued. "I'm resting after a long flight."

"Resting where? That monstrosity on Thornhill Road?" Her mother awaited a response. "That's right, Katherine. I know all about your purchase. Now why don't you come up to Greyabbey for dinner so we can discuss it."

Kit's stomach clenched. Her mother knew. She shouldn't be surprised, really. Heloise was more plugged in than electronics in an Apple store.

"And by discuss, you mean lecture me on all the reasons the purchase was a bad idea."

"Honestly, Katherine." To the untrained ear, it simply sounded like an exasperated mother. For Katherine, however, that single phrase was loaded with judgment.

"I'll be there for dinner."

"Excellent. No need to dress up, darling. Just a casual dinner for our little reunion. Maybe wear those pearls I bought you for graduation."

Pearls were her mother's idea of casual. "I'll be there in an hour."

"Forty minutes," her mother said. "You know you can't keep Diane's dishes waiting."

Because twenty minutes would make or break a meal. "Fine."

If there was one thing Kit knew well, it was that dinner at Greyabbey was never a casual affair.

At six o'clock Kit began the walk up Thornhill Road, praying that the front end of her sandals didn't get caught in the sidewalk cracks. She hoped her car arrived from Los Angeles soon because she didn't want to be trapped inside the four corners of Westdale any more than necessary.

On the way, she fished her phone from her purse and called Beatrice for an update.

"If it isn't my favorite college student." Beatrice's raspy voice crackled in the phone.

"Hi Bea. Any word on when my car will get here?"

"Should be with you this week."

Kit stepped over a stray branch in her path as she crossed Virginia Street and began the steep climb up Haverford Road.

"'This week' is kind of vague. Walking the streets of Westdale is not a good long-term option."

"Neither is living in Westdale, but it's what you need to do right now."

Kit inhaled sharply. "Any chance for a last minute reprieve? Maybe the ban's been lifted." Kit cringed as she said the words, knowing it was a long shot.

"Sorry, doll," Beatrice croaked. "You know I'd call you in a heartbeat if anything changed."

"I know." It was true. Beatrice only got paid if Kit got paid. The fact that Beatrice was keeping her on as a client, and a coveted one at that, was a testament to her loyalty. Kit hoped she could make it up to her with a huge paycheck one day.

"Are you huffing?" Beatrice asked in disbelief.

"And puffing," Kit admitted. Haverford Road was not an easy climb. "And if I could blow her house down, I would."

"You don't mean that," Beatrice scolded her. "Your mother is a legend."

"In her own mind," Kit replied. She was relieved to finally reach Winding Way, the premiere road in Westdale. If your house was located on Winding Way, it wasn't a house at all.

"She's donated to more pet charities in one year than Bill Gates gave to the entire continent of Africa."

"Stop checking out her financial records," Kit chastised her.

"I only look at the ones that are a matter of public record," Beatrice shot back. "I get dizzy seeing all those numbers in one long string."

Kit stopped at the gate and quickly ran a comb through her hair. She didn't want to give her mother any reason to criticize her. What was the point, though? If Kit showed up with a dozen angels on a cloud, her mother would question why they weren't playing harps.

"It's showtime, Bea."

"You're at your mother's?"

Kit gave a reluctant sigh. "Yep."

"Good luck, doll. I'm rooting for you."

"Bye." Kit dropped the phone into her purse and pressed the buzzer.

"Winthrop Wilder residence," a woman's voice said.

"Hi Diane. It's Kit."

"She's here," Diane exclaimed, presumably to other people in the room. "Okay, honey. Gate's open."

Kit pushed open the heavy metal door and strode up the pathway that led to Greyabbey. She only made it halfway when two Giant Schnauzers came tearing down the lawn toward her.

"Oh my gosh," Kit said, her eyes brimming with tears. She hadn't seen Hermes and Valentino in years. She held open her arms and Hermes leapt up, pushing her backward with his two front paws. Kit landed flat on her bottom in the grass, laughing as the dogs licked her face.

"Just as ladylike as I remember," a voice drawled.

Kit tugged her sundress down as she tried to extricate herself from the Giant Schnauzer wrestling moves.

"Huntley," Kit cried and scrambled to her feet to greet him. Technically, Huntley James was the household manager and Heloise's personal assistant. Unofficially, he was a second father to Kit. Originally from Georgia, Huntley embodied the charm and sophistication of the South in one cream linen suit and coordinating hat. His calming presence kept the Winthrop Wilder residence from descending into madness.

"You're a rose in full bloom," Huntley enthused, holding her at a distance for a better view. "The English climate suited you."

"I was only in London for three weeks," Kit said. "You can thank my trainer for how I look." Hans had taught her

11

everything from martial arts to shooting a bow and arrow. Pulling that bowstring was harder than it looked. She fought back a few tears, remembering that she'd never train with Hans again.

"Ah yes, the famous Hans," Huntley commented. She'd had regular contact with Huntley since she moved away so he knew all the relevant names.

Kit squinted up at Huntley. "You look good, too." At six foot three inches in stocking feet, he towered above the Winthrops and the Wilders. She touched his tan face. "Your hat's not doing its job, though."

"That color is the result of a little jaunt to Barbados," Huntley admitted. "Your mother's belated birthday gift to me." Heloise had always been generous with her staff, sending them on vacations and buying them expensive clothes and jewelry. Kit had to admit, her generosity inspired devotion.

Kit chewed her lip, afraid to ask her next question. "And how is my dear mother?"

"Step inside, my fair lady, and see for yourself." Huntley offered his arm and Kit linked through it as the dogs sniffed around her feet.

Kit eyed the grand house from the safety of the front lawn. It had been modeled after a French country estate with six bedrooms, seven fireplaces and the carriage house where Huntley lived.

"So is this a two martini dinner?" she asked.

Huntley shrugged. "You haven't been home in a few years. I'd wager three minimum."

Kit stepped into the familiar foyer where Diane awaited her with a toothy smile and a smothering hug. As the longtime housekeeper and cook, Diane had seen Kit through the awkward years of adolescence and the rebellious teen years. Not that Kit had been very rebellious then. Her act of treason was jetting off to Los Angeles to become an actress. A move her mother still resented, since Heloise painted television actors with the same brush as prostitutes and human rights activists.

"Diane," Kit choked, "I can't breathe."

Diane released Kit from her ample bosom. "You don't look a day older than the day you left, Kit."

"Right back at you." It was a lie, of course. Diane reminded Kit of a female version of Gimli, the dwarf warrior from Lord of the Rings. It didn't matter, though. Kit adored Diane warts and all and, in this case, the warts were not an idiom.

"Your mother's in her study," Diane said. "Would you like to see her?"

"Do I have a choice?" Kit whispered.

Diane leaned toward her. "No."

As Kit trailed behind Huntley and Diane, she heard the sound of birdsong coming from inside the house.

"Um, what is that noise?" Kit said, pausing to listen.

Huntley's brow wrinkled in confusion until the birdsong began again. He broke into a broad grin. "Oh yes, you hear Tiffany and Van Cleef. Your mother has acquired a number of new housemates in your absence."

Housemates. Kit was afraid to ask.

"Kit's here," Diane chirped when they arrived at her mother's study. Diane and Huntley promptly disappeared, leaving Kit alone in the doorway.

The chair swiveled around to reveal Heloise Winthrop Wilder, decked out in bright pink organza and sequins, stroking a white cat on her lap. Her mother's style was more flamboyant than the typical Westdale maven. Kit doubted that any other woman in town could get away with it.

"Katherine, darling. We're so relieved to have you home at last."

"Hello, Mother." Kit thought that her mother looked gaunter than when she'd last seen her. Her enviable cheekbones were more pronounced and her jawline more defined.

Heloise lifted the cat and carried her over to meet Kit halfway. They reached the center of the room at the same time. Three inches taller, Kit stooped slightly to kiss her mother's cheek. It was Heloise's preferred greeting.

"I said casual," Heloise remarked, surveying Kit's sundress and sandals. "Not Goodwill chic."

Kit glanced down at the pretty dress. "I wore this for a magazine shoot."

She touched the light fabric of the dress. "Well, I suppose that's the demographic they were aiming for. Poor people watch a lot of television."

Kit counted to three in her head, a technique she'd picked up in high school. No point in getting tossed out before she'd eaten.

"Who's the cat?" Kit asked.

Heloise thrust the cat into Kit's arms. "Miss Moneypenny, meet my daughter, Katherine."

"You named her after a movie character?" Kit scoffed. All the grief that Kit received as a result of Fool's Gold and here she was naming cats after Bond characters.

"She is named after a character in a novel," Heloise corrected her.

Kit reddened. She should have known better. The one thing she and her mother agreed on was their love of books. Although her father had spent a lot of time in the Greyabbey library, everyone knew the books really belonged to Heloise and Kit.

Kit rubbed behind Miss Moneypenny's ear and the cat purred loudly.

"Huntley found her wandering the country club golf course. She was so thin and sickly. He nearly struck her near the ninth hole."

Kit eyed the cat's fluffy white coat and healthy glow. "Well, you've done wonders for her. She looks healthy."

Heloise rubbed her nose against Miss Moneypenny's. "She is amazing. Yes, she is."

Kit bit back a sarcastic remark. In sixty seconds, Heloise had shown more affection for a stray cat than she'd ever shown for her daughter.

Heloise took the cat back from Kit. "Come along. We don't want to spoil Diane's sumptuous dinner by arriving late to the table."

They left the study and walked to the back of the house, entering the elegant dining room. Heloise took her place at the head of the table and settled the cat on her lap. Kit inhaled sharply when her mother plucked a water goblet from the table and offered it to Miss Moneypenny.

"Diane, this is Perrier, correct?" Heloise called, sniffing the water. "It smells a little like tap water and you know how I feel about that."

Kit sat to the left of her mother, struggling not to react. Tap water wasn't good enough for the cat?

"So how do you like the house on Thornhill?" Huntley asked, taking the seat opposite Kit.

Heloise narrowed her eyes. "Yes, do tell. Imagine my surprise when I heard that my unemployed daughter had purchased a house in Westdale."

Kit winced at the word 'unemployed.'

"I sold my place in L.A.," Kit explained. "Plus, I just finished a part in a British film."

"What about living expenses?" Heloise queried. "I offered to pay for college, not to reinstate your trust fund. Why wouldn't you just live here and save the money? It's not like we're short on space."

Kit knew it was only a matter of time before her trust fund was mentioned. Kit's mother had revoked the trust when Kit opted to pursue an acting career in Los Angeles. She had been extremely fortunate to snag the role of Ellie Gold right out of the gate. Otherwise, she'd have been waiting tables and auditioning like everyone else.

"The house has good bones and it was in foreclosure," Kit argued. "I saw it as an investment opportunity."

"Well, that would make your father proud," Heloise said, the obvious implication being that it didn't make her proud.

Huntley reached for the salad tongs. "I didn't think we had foreclosures in Westdale." Westdale was like a bubble of affluence, rarely pierced by the sharp pin of the real world. Huntley lived in the guest cottage on the estate. Other than vacations, he only left Greyabbey for visits to the country club and the occasional shopping trip to Liberty Square.

"The owner had money problems and ran off without paying his mortgage. It's not unusual." That was all Kit knew and, as far as she was concerned, that was all she needed to know. One man's burden of debt was an actress-turned-college student's golden opportunity.

"Now that you're here permanently," Heloise began, "it's high time you attend the next Pilgrim Society meeting." Heloise was the chairwoman of the Pilgrim Society, an organization for descendants of the first Pilgrims to arrive in the New World on the Mayflower. The Winthrops were descended from Isaac Allerton, one of the pious members of the group.

"Mother, you know I don't do Mayflower Madness."

"Really, darling? Madness. It's a lovely group of people upholding our longstanding Christian values."

"And by upholding, you mean talking about it and then completely doing the opposite, right? Because that's the way I remember it."

Heloise tipped the goblet toward Miss Moneypenny's water-seeking tongue. "Katherine, it's important to honor our legacy."

"I'll find another way to honor our legacy, thanks. Maybe I'll get lucky and pass a few stray cats on my way home."

Huntley's long leg shot underneath the table and Kit felt the pressure of his large foot on her toes. She pulled back, tucking her feet beneath her chair and trying not to sulk. She'd been living on her own for the past five years and in the span of one dinner, she'd been reduced to toddler behavior. Maybe a return to Westdale had been a bad idea after all.

The next day Kit took advantage of the morning sunshine by dragging the hideous blush carpet out onto the front lawn in strips. It was hard work, but Kit was determined to do it herself. Even with her brief stint in London, she'd felt fairly useless since losing her role on Fool's Gold. Manual labor kept her hands occupied and her mind off her uncertain future. She dropped another strip of nylon onto the grass and headed back inside for more.

"I recommend calling the borough to have them take the carpet away," a voice said.

Kit spun around to see a white-haired woman riding an electric scooter. "I was hoping to give it away rather than throw it away," Kit explained. "It still looks new."

The woman made an unpleasant sound. "Forget charity. You don't want to risk the wrath of Peregrine Monroe. Don't let the pearls fool you. That woman is lethal."

Kit blinked. "Who's Peregrine Monroe?" The name sounded familiar. With a moniker like Peregrine, she was likely someone who ran in her mother's circle.

"Your neighbor." The woman nodded to the house on the left on the corner of Keystone and Thornhill Roads.

Kit observed the well-groomed house beside hers. Every tree branch was perfectly straight and every blade of grass evenly cut. It was the home of an extremely tidy person.

"Why? Is she morally opposed to pink carpet?" Kit asked jokingly.

"If it's on the front lawn, then yes." The woman didn't crack a smile. "She complained bitterly about your predecessor and his beloved motor home. Have no doubt that she'll be filing a complaint if you give her half a reason."

"Thanks for the warning," Kit said. "I'm Kit Wilder, by the way."

"I recognize you. You have your mother's cheekbones. I'm Phyllis Chilton," the woman replied. "I live across the street, number fifty-three."

"Nice to meet you, Phyllis."

"Find anything good in there?"

"Like what?" Kit asked. "Buried treasure?"

Phyllis snorted. "Doubtful. If Ernie had treasure, it would've lasted five minutes before he spent it all."

"I guess that explains why his house was in foreclosure."

"The man liked betting on the Eagles more than he liked paying his mortgage."

"So where did he go?"

"Nobody knows for sure." Phyllis shrugged. "Can't say anybody cared either. He wasn't known for his sparkling personality."

"Well, I hope I'm an improvement then."

"There's your other neighbor now," Phyllis said, making a cuckoo sign with her finger. "Thora's a sweet girl. Helluva a green thumb, too. If she gives you any advice about your garden, take it."

Kit looked toward the house on her right. The sweet girl looked about eighty years old with cropped white hair and stooped shoulders. Thora waved and slowly made her way over to them.

"Well, hello," Thora said. "I wasn't sure when we'd actually get to meet you."

"Sorry, I've been busy with school and getting settled. I'm Kit Wilder."

"I've got your bling right here," Thora said in her gravelly voice and slapped her knee, laughing. "What a show. I loved that hunky co-star of yours. What was his name?"

"Charlie Owen," Kit said. "He played Jason, my boss and love interest."

Thora clapped her hands together. "Oh, what was it like, lip-smacking with him? What a dreamboat."

Kit resisted the urge to tell her that Charlie's breath regularly smelled of the garlic and onion bagel that he'd wolfed down for breakfast that morning followed by a cup of black coffee. During their brief, real-life fling, Kit had put the kibosh on his garlic bagel habit.

"He was great to work with," Kit said with a polite smile. Until he wasn't.

"I wouldn't leave this carpet here if I were you," Thora said.

"Yes, Phyllis mentioned the wrath of Peregrine."

Thora and Phyllis exchanged wary glances. "Don't get off on the wrong foot with her," Phyllis warned. "She's not an easy person to live next door to at the best of times."

Kit stared at the tangle of carpet at her feet and sighed. She didn't want to annoy her neighbor on day one. Politeness dictated that she should wait a month at least.

"Great. So who do I need to call to get rid of this mess?"

"I cannot believe Kit Wilder is about to sand her own floors," Jordan said, his angular face filling Kit's iPhone screen. Jordan hadn't believed that Kit was actually doing the work herself and had demanded a visual.

"Please don't report it to the tabloids," Kit warned. "Not even for fun." She could envision the headlines now — Desperate Actress Takes Job in Construction to Make Ends Meet.

"You're overthinking this, Kit Kat," Jordan advised. "People love to see celebs get their hands dirty. It makes you seem relatable. Go ahead and give your fans a good HGTV moment."

Kit surveyed the lighting in the room. With the natural sunlight streaming in through the open windows, the room did have an appealing glow.

"Okay, I'll do it," she agreed. "We both know it won't be the most unflattering photo ever posted of me."

She was referring to the slew of paparazzi pictures over the years that depicted her in various unattractive guises such as leaving the gym dripping with sweat, on a morning coffee run with her hair unbrushed, and her favorite one — chewing food in a restaurant.

"You should wear the gift I sent you," Jordan advised. "It'll come in handy when the dust starts flying."

"Your gift," she echoed, remembering the package that had been waiting for her. "What's in the box, Jordan?" Now her suspicion was aroused.

"I may have swiped a few items from the set for you," he said with a casual air. "You deserve a few keepsakes."

Kit walked over to the mantle and opened the lid.

"Oh Jordan, you shouldn't have." She pulled a roll of yellow crime scene tape from the box.

"I thought you might want to decorate with it," he said. "Or bring it with you to your mother's house in case WASP-y tensions run high."

"When tensions run high, we reach for the decanter, not the kitchen knife." She set aside the tape and peered back into the box. "No way, you did not steal this for me."

"Am I your best friend or what?"

Kit removed a gas mask that she'd worn in season two of Fool's Gold. She pulled the mask over her head and held up the phone.

"Luke, I am your father," she breathed heavily, doing her best Darth Vader impression. She turned the phone around and snapped her photo before turning back to Jordan.

"Emmy nominee Kit Wilder, ladies and gentleman," he said in his best announcer voice. "Post it now so I can leave a snarky comment."

Kit swiped her way to Instagram and posted the photo with the caption — 'A new role as a Dalek or DIY in my new house. You decide.'

Kit removed the mask and placed it back in the box. "Thanks, Jordan. I think I will wear it during the sanding process." She took a good look at the oak floorboards. It was going to be a tough job, but she knew the floors would be beautiful when they were finished. She liked the idea of restoring the room to its former glory. As far as Kit was concerned, Ernie Ludwig didn't give the house the respect it deserved.

"Edit the Dalek part. Most of your followers won't get the reference," he told her.

"Dr. Who is iconic," she insisted.

"To you and me, maybe. Not to the masses."

"Am I supposed to fill the gaps before or after I sand?" Kit asked, spying a crack between boards.

"Um, definitely the kind of thing you should know before you start," Jordan pointed out. "How big is the gap? If it's not big enough to lose a foot in, you might want to leave it. Gaps in the floorboards add character."

Kit crossed the room to inspect the flooring. "I don't think I want to leave this one. It ruins the look." She crouched down and held the phone so that Jordan could see.

"I see what you mean," he said. "It actually looks like somebody pulled it up but didn't put it back properly." He clapped his hands giddily. "You should take a peek. Maybe someone hid money there. People did that in days of yore."

"I don't think last century qualifies as days of yore." Either way, Kit doubted that Ernie hid any money there. From what the neighbors said, he didn't have any money to hide.

"No, those were the days of yawn, except the Eighties. That decade is epic."

"Hold on a sec," Kit said. "Let me grab my hammer."

Jordan laughed. "I love hearing you utter statements like that. It's surreal."

Kit stuck out her tongue before retrieving the hammer from the nearby toolbox. She used the curved end to pull up the crooked floorboard.

"Wow, brute strength," Jordan remarked. "You've still got it, babe."

"I'm going to hang up on you," Kit threatened.

"And ruin the suspense? I'll be good. I promise."

Kit eased the board from its secure position so as not to damage it further. "What on earth…" She peered down at the disturbing contents.

"Is it gold?" Jordan asked eagerly. "Fool's Gold," he added, chuckling to himself.

"Definitely not gold of any kind," Kit replied, holding the phone over the opening. Jordan's shriek of terror pierced her eardrum.

"Great Mother of Pearl," Jordan gasped. "Please tell me it's a chew toy for a Rhodesian Ridgeback."

Kit stared at the well-preserved bones. "If only." She'd need to pull up more floorboards to uncover the rest of the skeleton. She placed the phone next to her knee and picked up the hammer. As she began to pop off another floorboard, she heard Jordan cry out.

"What are you doing?" he yelled. "Don't tamper with evidence. Call the police."

"I just want to make sure it is what I think it is," Kit explained. She didn't want to be the laughingstock of her new neighborhood if she was mistaken. She'd been humiliated enough for one lifetime.

"You're not going to touch it, are you?"

"When did you become such a baby?" Kit asked. "We touched weird things on set all the time."

"Fake things," Jordan clarified. "Not actual human remains."

Kit bit her lip. "I guess four years in television desensitized me." She studied the bones for a moment. "I'll call you back when I'm done." Before he could object, she tapped the phone and his face disappeared.

Kit methodically removed each floorboard until the entire skeleton was visible. Yep, definitely human and, amazingly, all in one piece. Someone went to a lot of trouble to hide it. She noticed that the chest wall was concave, as though something heavy had been forced into it or pressed on top of it but didn't actually break the bones. Unless there were hairline fractures she couldn't see. Whatever caused this type of damage was probably the murder weapon. She was fairly certain one of the neighbors would have noticed a battering ram making its way through the neighborhood, though. Kit's thoughts shifted to the neighbors. They certainly didn't have anything nice to say about Ernie Ludwig. Disliked, debt-ridden Ernie Ludwig who disappeared without a trace. Kit stared at the skeleton.

"Ernie?" she whispered.

Jordan was right. It was time to call the Westdale police.

Chapter Two

Rich Riley, Westdale's chief of police, stood in Kit's living room flanked by two police officers as they examined the skeleton. The two young police officers seemed more excited by Kit's presence than the presence of a murder victim.

"Do you remember that episode where you went undercover as the clown?" the shorter officer asked.

"It's hard not to remember all the episodes when you're actually in them," Kit said. "What's your name again?"

"Lucas. Officer Harley." He straightened and puffed out his puny chest.

"Brian Jamison," the redheaded officer added, not to be left out of the introduction.

Kit glanced at the chief. Was it Take Your Sons to Work Day? Even to someone as young as Kit, these two didn't seem old enough — or smart enough — to be crime fighters.

"Boys, let's focus on the task at hand," Chief Riley said, snapping his fingers impatiently.

Reluctantly, the officers tore their attention away from Kit.

"I hate to tell you this since you just moved in," Chief Riley said to Kit, "but your living room is now a crime scene."

Kit's shoulders slumped. "Can I stay in my house if I stay out of the living room?"

"Let's wait and see what the detective says," Chief Riley replied. "He's on his way now."

Kit hoped that they allowed her to stay in the house. The last thing she wanted was a reason to return to Greyabbey. She didn't want to see her mother's smug expression.

"If you have somewhere to be, you're welcome to leave while we work," the chief said.

"I had a date with a floor sander," Kit said. "I guess that's cancelled." She glanced longingly at the equipment on the far side of the room.

"Jamison, where's the crime scene tape?" Chief Riley boomed. "We need to seal off the area."

Kit saw the fear in Officer Jamison's eyes and realized that he didn't bring the tape. She jogged over to the mantle where she'd left the present from Jordan.

"Here it is," she said brightly and handed the roll to Jamison.

His confusion was evident but he accepted the tape without question. "I'm on it, Chief."

"This must be pretty interesting if the Chief was unchained from his desk," a deep voice said.

Kit turned to see a tall, olive-skinned man in a light gray suit step into the living room. His hair was dark and wavy, the kind that begged a girl to run her fingers through it.

"Romeo, Romeo, wherefore art thou," Officer Harley said.

"Gee, I never heard that one before," Mr. Tall, Dark and Handsome replied.

27

"Detective Moretti." Chief Riley greeted him with a firm handshake.

"I knew it was serious when you called," Detective Moretti said, eyeing the skeleton.

"Romeo, do you know who this is?" Harley asked, gesturing to Kit.

"The unsuspecting homeowner?" Romeo ventured.

"Besides that," Jamison chimed in.

Romeo gave Kit a cursory glance. "No, should I?"

"Fool's Gold," Harley prompted. "Detective Ellie Gold. I got your bling right here." Kit recognized a diehard fan when she heard one. He mimicked Kit's delivery perfectly.

Romeo's mouth quirked. "Sounds like an interesting show."

"Interesting?" Harley scoffed. "It was required viewing in our house. We don't watch it anymore."

"I don't watch TV period," Romeo said.

"I told you he's a weirdo," Harley told Jamison. "He probably only watches Rocky DVDs." He turned to Kit. "We were supremely pissed when you got killed off, by the way. I even signed the petition to bring you back."

Kit managed a smile. "Thanks."

"Why'd they kill you off?" Romeo asked, seemingly intrigued. "Salary dispute?"

"More like a personality dispute," she replied vaguely.

Romeo suppressed a grin.

"Could I interrupt this breaking entertainment news and get back to our murder victim?" Chief Riley said. "I think it goes without saying that Ernie Ludwig needs our attention more than Miss Wilder does."

"That's the name of our vic?" Romeo asked.

28

"He's the former owner of this house," Harley said. "He disappeared last year and the house went into foreclosure. I guess the bank didn't empty the house completely after all."

"Rumor had it that he ran off because he owed a lot of money," Jamison added. "Guess he didn't get very far."

Kit listened to the exchange with interest. The entire scene felt comfortably familiar — it was almost like being back on set. As far as she knew, Ernie owed money to the bank. It was unlikely that the bank would send thugs to remind Ernie of his debts. So that meant that Ernie owed money to other people besides the bank or that his death was unrelated to his debts. She thought of her neighbor, Peregrine Monroe, and wondered whether she was the type of woman who would kill a man over a messy yard. Kit decided there was only one way to find out.

Kit wandered the bucolic grounds of Westdale College, killing time before first-year orientation. She had fond memories of the campus. Despite the extensive grounds at Greyabbey, her father had often brought her here to play catch or attend the lecture of a notable visiting professor. He wanted her to expand her horizons and not get so comfortable in life that she became complacent. Well, he'd be happy with her progress on that score.

She settled on a bench in front of Warren Fountain, enjoying the tickle of a breeze on the nape of her neck. The day was warm and humid, typical for late August. She'd pulled her hair back into a slick ponytail in an effort to beat the heat but also blend in. During her brief time back in

Westdale, she noticed that the classic ponytail was alive and thriving here.

The fountain was built in the style of an in-ground pool with a large, abstract sculpture shooting out of the middle. Kit thought it resembled an alien tree, silver and sparkling in the sunlight.

Kit watched two girls chatting and laughing as they walked toward Plymouth Hall. Their blond ponytails swatted each other as they bounced their way past the fountain. Kit thought the girl on the left was perilously close to the edge. She opened her mouth to call out, but then snapped it shut. The girl wasn't blind; clearly she could see how close she was. It quickly became apparent that she couldn't.

As one foot disappeared into the water, Kit shot off the bench before the girl had time to yell. Kit grabbed her arm and pulled her sideways to prevent her from falling in. Then she said a silent thank you to Hans for her rescue training.

"Omigod, you're like a superhero," the girl exclaimed, her cheeks bright pink with embarrassment.

"I told you not to walk so close to it," the other girl scolded her. She glanced at Kit. "Charlotte is dyspraxic. That means her proprioception is compromised. Do you know what that is? Most people don't. Basically, she always needs to be aware of her surroundings or she's likely to fall into a ditch."

Kit blinked. The girl's rapid response managed to sound both intelligent and confusing.

"You look familiar," Charlotte, the ditch-faller, said.

"You do," the other girl agreed, her blond ponytail bobbing.

"I'm Kit Wilder," she told them, awaiting the usual response.

"You're Heloise Winthrop Wilder's daughter," the one-who-was-not-Charlotte said, her blue eyes brightening. "Oh, and you were on television. A prime time network show, not cable."

"I was. 'Was' being the crucial word in that statement," Kit said.

"I'm Francie Musgrove and this is Charlotte Tilton. We're on our way to orientation."

"So am I," Kit said. "Part of my penance for disobeying my mother and running off to join the Hollywood circus is attending Westdale College."

"It is the college of choice for useless spares," Charlotte said, her nose scrunching. "You're not a spare, are you?"

"No, I'm an only child," Kit said. "But still useless."

Charlotte nodded toward the fountain. "Not completely. I'd have been soaked and mortified if you hadn't come along."

"Wouldn't have been the first time," Francie muttered.

"Would you mind if I went in with you?" Kit asked. "I don't know anyone. In case you hadn't done the math, I'm a little older than the average first year."

Francie beamed. "We wouldn't mind escorting a bonafide star into the room. Our stock will skyrocket."

"Not that we'd only do it because you're part Winthrop," Charlotte added quickly.

Kit wasn't bothered either way. As far as she was concerned, she needed friends right now more than she needed to prove her independence. Together, the trio

31

entered Plymouth Hall to kick off the first day of their college experience.

Kit rang the bell of the pretty Dutch Colonial house. No chipped paint, no weeds — everything was in perfect order. The door opened to reveal a slight woman in a coral twin set and neatly pressed slacks. Her brown hair was styled in a chin-length bob and she wore an elegant pearl necklace with matching earrings. It seemed that Peregrine Monroe herself was also in perfect order.

"Hi, you must be my new neighbor," Kit said, turning on the charm. "I'm Kit Wilder."

Peregrine gave her a haughty look. "Yes, of course. The Winthrop Wilder girl who ran off and joined the circus. I know all about you."

"It wasn't a circus," Kit objected. Someone clearly worshipped the same society gods as Heloise Winthrop Wilder.

Peregrine narrowed her hazel eyes. "I beg to differ." She stepped aside. "Do come in."

"Thank you." Kit stepped into the entry hall and was struck by the Spartan interior. Peregrine Monroe seemed like a person who had belongings. Her house suggested otherwise. It looked barely lived in.

"I'm downsizing," Peregrine said, noting Kit's surprise.

"Oh." Kit hadn't heard that the house was for sale. "Where are you planning to move?"

"Sedona, to be closer to my sister."

"I guess we won't be neighbors very long then."

"Can I offer you a drink? An iced tea, perhaps?" Peregrine looked hopeful that Kit would decline. Naturally, she accepted.

"An iced tea would be divine," she said with a big smile.

Peregrine's own smile tightened as she made her way to the kitchen. Kit trailed behind her, checking out each room they passed. Not a battering ram in sight.

"Have you been planning this move for a long time?" Kit asked. Either Peregrine hadn't owned much to begin with or she'd been slowly and steadily packing away her belongings in anticipation of the big day.

"No," Peregrine replied, pouring homemade iced tea from a glass pitcher into a tall glass. "Not that I could've gone anywhere while that horrid Ernie Ludwig lived next door. He was single-handedly destroying my property value."

Kit sipped her iced tea. "I heard he wasn't winning any Neighbor of the Year awards."

"I should think not," Peregrine scoffed. "I was thrilled to hear that someone from a respectable family had bought the house. It was serendipity. Now I can list my house for sale with no worries."

A minute ago she'd run off and joined the circus. Now she was respectable? It seemed the Winthrop Wilder name was still valuable currency in Westdale.

"You may want to put a hold on that listing," Kit advised and told her about the grim discovery.

"I didn't hear any sirens," Peregrine replied, gazing out the rear window.

"I doubt sirens were necessary given that the corpse was a skeleton."

Peregrine's lips puckered. "Oh no," she said. "A murder next door. This won't do at all. I hope they intend to keep this quiet. If people find out, my house will never sell."

Kit had just told her that her missing neighbor's bones had been discovered in the house next door and her main concern was the sale of her house. And she'd thought Hollywood was heartless. What was the world coming to?

"I understand that you really disliked Ernie," Kit said casually.

"Of course I disliked him. He was a menace to the neighborhood."

Menacing enough to murder? "I heard you filed official complaints."

"No more than Thora did," Peregrine said.

Kit's eyebrows shot up. Thora? The elderly woman hadn't mentioned making any complaints. "What did Thora complain about?"

"His ghastly motor home, of course. The worst part was that he never used it. If you have a second home, it should be somewhere like Martha's Vineyard, for heaven's sake, not your driveway. It sat there most of the year and blocked the sunlight to Thora's prizewinning rose bushes. She couldn't grow anything decent once he'd bought that monstrosity."

Kit's mind was spinning. Why hadn't Thora mentioned it? Why hadn't Peregrine told the other neighbors she was planning to sell her house?

Kit finished her iced tea. "Well, the police are in my house now and I suspect it will get busier over there before the day is over. You may want to seek refuge at the country club or something."

Peregrine gazed out the kitchen window and sighed. "If I had my druthers, I'd be seeking refuge in Sedona right now."

After her fruitful visit with Peregrine, the number of people populating her front lawn dissuaded Kit from returning to her house. It was almost as bad as paparazzi.

She turned right instead of left and headed to Liberty Square on foot. She really needed her car. According to Beatrice's latest report, it was somewhere in Ohio. Thankfully, the air was warm and pleasant and it would give Kit a chance to process what she'd learned from Peregrine.

The high-energy sound of It's Raining Men jolted her and she pulled her phone from her handbag.

"Hallelujah," she sang into the phone.

"I told you to stop using that for my ring tone," Jordan complained. "It's trite."

"Fine, I'll change it to Ain't No Mountain High Enough."

"You never called me back," he said. "I thought you might have been buried beneath the floorboards, too."

"Sorry, it got crazy once the police arrived. My house is officially a crime scene."

"You must feel perfectly at home then," Jordan said.

Kit laughed. "I do, actually. Is that weird that I find it comforting? The sound of sirens and crime scene tape are my white noise."

"Glad your present came in handy."

"I know, right. You should see these cops, though. The word 'keystone' doesn't do them justice."

Kit passed the library and considered stopping in to register for a library card. She'd need to show residency, though. Maybe another time when she had paperwork available.

"Is someone chasing you? What's with the heavy breathing?" Jordan asked.

"I'm walking to Butter Beans."

"You need to up your exercise regime if you're panting from that. I was hoping it was because you'd seen a really hot guy."

Kit smiled into the phone. "As it happens, I did meet a super scorching guy today. Guess what his name is?"

"Robert Downey, Jr."

"Try again."

"Tom Cruise."

"I said super scorching, not super crazy." She turned right onto Standish Street. "Romeo. The hot detective on the case is called Romeo."

"He's the detective?" Jordan queried. "Girl, it's like Charlie Owen all over again."

"It is nothing like Charlie Owen," Kit bristled. She had nothing more to say on the subject. "I'm getting a well-deserved latte now. I'll call you later."

"But…" Jordan began. Kit turned off the phone and dropped it back into the deep chasm of her handbag. She needed a few minutes of peace and quiet.

She stepped inside Butter Beans and was relieved to see that the place was close to empty. Butter Beans had been a place she liked to hang out after school with friends.

Looking around at the cozy interior, Kit decided that the space was as warm and welcoming as she remembered.

Stepping up to the counter to place her order, she was greeted by a dough-faced barista. His nametag read 'Sam.'

"Hi Sam," she said. "I'd like a skinny vanilla latte, please."

"I got your latte right here," Sam said, doing his best Ellie Gold impression.

Kit smiled politely.

"See what I did there?" Sam asked. "With latte?"

Kit nodded. "I did see. Clever."

"I heard you found Ernie Ludwig," Sam said, lowering his voice.

News traveled at lightning speed in Westdale. "How is it possible that you know that?" Kit replied, glancing around the coffee shop for signs of a Westdale police officer.

Sam shrugged. "We're the official hub of Westdale information."

"My mother might disagree with that," Kit murmured.

"Since you're here, would it be okay if I asked you to look at my script?" Sam asked, pulling a thick ream of paper from a nearby messenger bag.

"Your script?" Kit echoed.

"When I heard you were moving back to Westdale, I started bringing my script to work just in case I ran into you. I heard you used to hang out here."

Great, even baristas in Westdale, Pennsylvania were aspiring screenwriters. "What's it about?" Kit asked.

Sam's pudgy face lit up. "This one's totally different. It'll blow your mind." He paused for dramatic effect. "Three words. Cowboys. In. Space."

"Like Serenity?" Kit asked.

Sam blinked. "What's Serenity?"

"What's Serenity?" Kit sucked in a breath. "Ever hear of a guy called Joss Whedon?"

"Sure. The Avengers guy, right?"

"Well, he didn't start with The Avengers. Do yourself a favor and check out his backlist."

Sam nodded eagerly. "Definitely. Anything you say."

Kit sighed inwardly with relief when she saw the script drop back into his bag. He set to work on her latte and she gratefully accepted the steaming mug. She maneuvered her way around the tables and chairs until she reached a plush chair by the window. Peace and quiet at last.

"Is this seat taken?" a voice asked.

Kit glanced up into the dark, dreamy eyes of Detective Romeo Moretti. "Shouldn't you be out there detecting?"

He shrugged and settled into the chair across from her. "I seem to have left my magnifying glass at home today."

She sipped her latte and it burned the tip of her tongue. She'd need to remember that Sam made scalding hot lattes.

"So will I be able to actually live in my new house?" she asked hopefully.

"Not yet, I'm afraid. The bones have been removed, but there's a lot more work to do. If you give me your cell number, I'll call you when we're finished."

For a moment, Kit wondered whether there was another reason he'd asked for her number but chalked it up to wishful thinking.

"A neighbor mentioned that you'd removed the living room carpet recently," he said.

"It was a crime against good taste," she said and then winced. The man was investigating a murder in her house and she was making jokes. Classy.

"It may contain evidence," Romeo said. "Where'd you put it?"

"I called the borough to have it taken it away," Kit said. "Phyllis and Thora warned me that Peregrine would have a cow if I left it too long on the front lawn for the world to see."

Romeo looked thoughtful. "Phyllis Chilton, Thora Breckenridge and Peregrine Monroe."

"Impressive," Kit said.

"I have a good memory. It helps with my detecting."

"What color are my eyes?" she asked and squeezed her eyes shut.

"Blue," he replied without missing a beat. "With gold flecks. Pretty."

Kit opened her eyes and smiled. "Very impressive." And smooth. Kit may not have committed any crimes, but looking at the handsome detective across from her, she knew she was definitely in trouble.

Chapter Three

By the time Kit arrived home, the officers on her front lawn had been replaced by neighbors and other nosy Westdale residents.

"We thought something had happened to you," Phyllis said, rolling toward Kit on her scooter.

"Not me," Kit said. "Your old neighbor."

Phyllis nodded solemnly. "Ernie was a jackass, but may he rest in peace."

Kit noticed a woman standing on the sidewalk with two metal forearm crutches. "Who's that?"

Phyllis craned her neck. "Adelaide Pye. She lives at the far end, on the corner of Thornhill and Virginia Street."

"Why does she have crutches?"

"Car accident," Phyllis said quietly. "Best thing that ever happened to her, really. She was a nasty piece of work before that. No one could tolerate her. Now that she's maimed, she's everybody's friend."

"Says the woman in the electric scooter," Kit said wryly.

"I can walk." Phyllis raised her chin a fraction. "I just choose not to."

"Will you choose to walk if I invite you inside to see where I found the skeleton?"

Phyllis's eyes lit up. "Would you?"

Kit nodded. "Quickly, I need to collect a few things before I decamp to Greyabbey."

Phyllis put her fingers to her lips and let out a shrieking whistle. "Thora," Phyllis called. "Come on over. We've got an invite."

Kit saw Thora step out from behind her thriving rose bushes. What a difference a year without a motor home made.

The two older women gave the other gawkers a victory sign with their fingers as they made their way into Kit's house.

Kit went straight to the living room. There was no need to point. The location was obvious now that the police had been there. More floorboards were ripped up and the house was far messier than Kit had left it. She picked up an empty Coke can in disgust.

"Okay, seriously. They can at least take their own trash with them," Kit huffed. "Can I get you ladies a drink? Hot tea?" Kit knew from childhood that older ladies in Westdale liked their hot tea.

"Yes, please," Thora answered.

Phyllis and Thora stood perfectly still, staring at the gaping hole where the body had been buried.

"That could have been either one of us," Phyllis murmured.

"Do you two have outstanding debt?" Kit asked.

They shook their heads mutely.

"Do people hate you?" Kit asked.

They shook their heads again.

"Then it couldn't have been either one of you," Kit said simply and turned to find where the kettle had been stashed in the kitchen. There were unpacked boxes everywhere she stepped, but she'd already unearthed the kettle the day before.

Fifteen minutes later the three women sat at the small, round table by the sliding glass door, discussing Ernie.

"I have to admit I'm relieved," Thora said. "I've been so frazzled since he disappeared. I've had horrible dreams about him this past year, riding on top of his motor home like it was a wild buffalo, trying to run me down. I even saw visions of him when I went to visit my daughter in Naples in the spring. Can you imagine?" She shook her head in dismay and set down her cup. "Not that I'm happy to learn he's dead, you know. But maybe now I'll stop imagining him."

"You had dreams that you were Ronald Reagan's mistress, too," Phyllis said. "His death didn't stop you."

"I have been known to have prescient dreams," Thora insisted. "My mother used to say I took after my Aunt Hazel who was well-known for her third eye."

"That's a psychic thing, not a deformity," Phyllis whispered to Kit. "Thora's batty as hell, but she's not in-bred."

"I heard that," Thora said. "I'm batty as hell, not deaf."

"I told Peregrine about the body," Kit said.

Both sets of eyes widened.

"What did she say?" Phyllis asked. "Did she confess?"

Kit laughed and sipped her tea. "Not exactly. Did you know she's planning to move to Sedona?"

"Her sister lives there," Phyllis said. "They're both widowed now. I guess they want to live nearer to each other."

"Peregrine mentioned something about your rose bushes," Kit said, eyeing Thora suspiciously. "Why didn't you tell me that you complained about his motor home?"

"Who are you, the fuzz?" Thora asked.

"Not anymore," Kit said.

"Not ever," Phyllis pointed out.

"Either way, I'm surprised you didn't mention it."

"Why would I complain about my old neighbor to my new neighbor?" Thora bristled. "It's impolite."

Thora had a point.

"Nobody on the street liked looking at that beast in his driveway," Phyllis said. "It bothered everyone, not just Thora and Peregrine."

Kit eyed Phyllis. "So it bothered you?"

Phyllis leaned forward and met Kit's gaze. "Of course it bothered me. It was an eyesore. A giant motor home on a bucolic street. He may as well have put a rusty Chevy up on bricks and called it a day."

Kit realized that she'd need to be mindful of her neighbors in Westdale. Not that she planned to drag down property values single-handedly.

"I hate to interrupt the society tea," Officer Jamison said, poking his head into the kitchen. "But you ladies aren't supposed to be here. You need to get going." He pointed to Kit. "That includes you, Officer Gold."

Kit began to clear the table. "Yes, sir."

"Thanks for the tape, by the way," he said. "It's my first real crime scene."

"You don't say," Kit replied, feigning surprise.

"Ms. Chilton, can I help you out?" he offered.

43

Phyllis stood in an effort to demonstrate her electric. "No, thank you. You just go about your business here so our neighbor can move back in. It'll be a nice change, having a neighbor we don't need to pretend we don't see."

"Give it time, Phyllis," Thora advised. "She's only just arrived."

Kit walked up the long lane to Greyabbey, rolling a suitcase of her belongings behind her. She wouldn't put it past her mother to have staged the entire incident in order to force Kit back into her controlling arms.

A flash of white linen caught her attention. Huntley lingered outside with the dogs, presumably awaiting Kit's arrival.

"Is it true, Sassafras?" he asked.

"All true," she said. "I'm sure my mother is finding the whole thing mildly amusing."

"Dr. Nina is with her now."

Kit started. "Is she ill?"

Huntley patted her back. "I forget you've been away. No, Dr. Nina is the local vet. She comes by once a week, barring any emergencies, to check on the menagerie. Jade is in kidney failure so Dr. Nina is here to change the drip."

Kit's nose wrinkled. "Which one is Jade?"

"That hairball with eyes called a Maine Coon. Terrible temper but your mother is overly fond of her."

Kit found it incredible that her mother doled out her particular brand of patient love to every stray animal within the Westdale town limits.

She located her mother in one of the lesser-used parlor rooms. The room was much altered since Kit's last visit. It looked like a makeshift animal hospital now.

"Katherine, welcome home," Heloise said, one hand placed protectively on Jade's back. "Dr. Nina, this is my daughter."

"It's only temporary," Kit warned. "As soon as the police have finished, I'm going back."

Heloise smiled. "Well, you've timed it just right. It's almost gin o'clock."

Dr. Nina closed her bag. "And that's my cue to leave. Nice to meet you, Katherine. I'm sure we'll see each other again soon."

"I'll escort her out," Huntley offered.

"Then fetch my popsicles," Heloise ordered.

Did she say popsicles? They were a bit beneath Heloise's culinary snobbery.

As if reading her mind, Heloise added, "They're cucumber and gin with white currants."

Ah, gin-based popsicles. Now that made more sense.

"Are you sure it won't spoil my dinner?" Kit asked.

"Oh Katherine, you're such a card. No amount of gin could possibly spoil a meal."

They enjoyed their gin-based popsicles on the veranda overlooking a courtyard garden. Kit begrudgingly accepted the fact that her mother's experiment had paid off. The popsicle was both decadent and delicious.

"There's a Pilgrim Society meeting next week that you should attend," Heloise said, managing to appear elegant as she licked the icy concoction. "If nothing else, it's a good way to meet eligible bachelors."

"You mean appropriate bachelors," Kit corrected her. "If they're in the Pilgrim Society, then they've already been vetted. Right, Mother?"

Heloise sucked her popsicle thoughtfully. "You say it as though there's something wrong with it."

Kit focused on the nearby butterfly in an effort to control her temper. "I don't need to meet any Westdale men stamped with your approval."

"Katherine, you really need to consider your age. A woman's childbearing years are fleeting."

"Then maybe you should've been more ambitious in your youth." She clucked her tongue disapprovingly. "Imagine the number of little Pilgrims you could have produced."

Kit caught the brief look of anger that flashed in her mother's clear blue eyes.

"Alas, you, Katherine darling, are my legacy." She finished off her popsicle and set the stick on a nearby cloth napkin. "Now you understand why it's so important that you accept the mantle of responsibility that comes with the Winthrop Wilder names."

Kit shrugged. "Do I?"

Huntley stepped onto the veranda, dabbing his forehead with a spotted handkerchief. "My sincere apologies for my tardiness, ladies. Crispin called about the next Pilgrim Society meeting and you know how that boy can talk."

That boy was Crispin Winthrop — Kit's first cousin who ran the local newspaper, the Westdale Gazette.

"Indeed, I do," Heloise replied as Huntley took a seat on the settee. "If you attend the meeting, next week, it might be a good opportunity to say hello to your family."

"Or I can swing by the paper," Kit suggested. "His office is right next to campus." Check and mate, she thought to herself.

"So tell me about school," Heloise suggested.

"Not much to tell. We're still doing orientation," Kit replied.

"Let me know if you have any issues and I'll speak to Josiah." Dr. Josiah Sorenson was the president of the college and a former golf buddy of Kit's father.

"I don't need you to solve my problems," Kit said.

"You seem to have so many," Heloise said. "I'd just like to lighten the load."

"Dinner is served," Diane called from inside.

"What does she think this is, a Friendly's?" Heloise remarked. "She must be acting up for your benefit." She shot an accusative glare in Kit's direction.

Kit stood on the edge of the pasture, her gaze fixed on the Tennessee walking horse with its head lowered to the ground. Peppermint had always loved sniffing the daisies; it was something that Kit adored about her horse. She was a magnificent creature still.

"Hey girl," Kit called and the horse's head rose in response, her ears twitching.

Kit approached the horse slowly, not wanting to startle her. She held out the apple in her palm and watched Peppermint for signs of interest.

"Apples are still her favorite," a voice said, "if that's what you're wondering."

Kit turned around to see an unfamiliar young man behind her. His scrawny body was emphasized by his thin T-shirt and jeans. He wore a red Phillies cap, a familiar sight in this part of Pennsylvania.

"Hi, are you the stablehand?" Kit asked.

"Paul Krasensky. I started working here about two years ago."

"That explains why you don't look familiar." Kit returned her attention to Peppermint. "How is she?"

"Give her that apple and you'll see for yourself," he suggested.

Kit held the apple within reach and Peppermint took it, chomping gingerly.

"Watch, it'll be like a sugar high in a minute. She loves her apples, especially Pink Lady and Gala."

Kit warmed to him immediately. A stablehand who knew the brand of apples her horse liked. Now that was a good employee. "Did Abe train you?" The family's previous stablehand, Abe, had retired while Kit was in Los Angeles so she wasn't sure of the timeframe.

"Yep, my older brother used to shoot pool with him before the old guy's hip surgery so he recommended me for the job."

"Who's your brother?" Kit searched her brain for another Krasensky. "Does he work here, too?"

Paul shook his head. "Nah. Carl works odd jobs. He isn't a big fan of steady employment, if you know what I mean. Ain't seen him in some time." He spat on the ground. "Not unusual for my family, though. Too many

48

Krasenskys spoil the broth. Someone should've warned my mama about that before she went and had six kids."

Kit smiled, stroking the horse's soft mane. "Sometimes even one is enough."

"I like your mama," Paul said, surprising her. "Anybody who takes care of animals the way she does is okay in my book."

Kit didn't argue. Most people assumed that Heloise's nurturing side extended to her daughter. Her mother was an enigma, though, and Kit gave up trying to figure her out years ago.

"You want me to saddle her for you?" Paul asked.

"Not today," Kit said. "Thanks. I just wanted to say hello. I've missed her." She placed her nose close to Peppermint's, breathing in her earthy scent.

"Well, she gets attention. Don't you worry about that. Your mama's down here pretty often."

Kit's eyes popped. "My mother? Out here?" As much as Heloise loved her menagerie, Kit's horse was pretty far down the list. She tended to stick with animals she could confine and control within the four walls of Greyabbey. One of the reasons that Kit failed to qualify.

Paul shoved his hands in his pockets, sensing he said something wrong. "She's a real stickler. Makes sure Peppermint is getting plenty of exercise and what not."

"Huh." Kit didn't know what to say. "Well, I'm back now and I intend to spend quality time with her."

"I'll bet your mama will be real happy about that."

Kit's brow creased. "I'm talking about Peppermint."

"Oh. 'Course you are." He fell silent and Kit gave Peppermint one last pat before heading back to the house.

"It was nice meeting you, Paul."

"See you around, Miss Wilder."

"Call me Kit. Everyone else does."

"Everyone except your mama. I ain't never heard her call you nothing but Katherine."

Kit glanced at him sharply before trudging back to Greyabbey for the evening. Sadly, 'everyone except her mama' pretty much summed up her entire life.

Kit slid into a seat at the back of the room, hoping no one noticed her lateness. The walk from Greyabbey had taken longer than expected and then she'd gotten lost in the building and ended up in an anthropology class. When she saw Francie and Charlotte's matching blond ponytails, she knew she was in the right place.

To her relief, she'd received a text that morning that her car would be delivered to Greyabbey that afternoon. Small favors and all that.

"The human experience. The study of how people think, behave and feel. That's why we're here. That's psychology." Professor Wentworth worked the room like a talk show host. He had charisma, Kit acknowledged. He was also easy on the eyes, although the hot pink tie suggested that she might not be his type. She snapped a surreptitious photo of him during the lecture and sent it to Jordan for his input. Not that she was interested in dating a professor. More negative press was the last thing she needed. Leaving Los Angeles was hard enough. Throw a corpse and a forbidden relationship on top of that and you had yourself one humdinger of a reputation. Kit was already the engine of the gossip train. She didn't need to be the caboose, too.

Jordan's reply was short and sweet. "Not all pink ties are created equal. He's one of yours. Too bad." He added a sad face emoji for good measure.

Kit stifled a giggle.

"All phones should be turned off and tucked away," Professor Wentworth said loudly, shooting a pointed look in Kit's direction.

The heat rose to her cheeks and Kit turned off the phone before sliding it into her bag. She'd need to get reacquainted with school rules. It had been a few years since they'd applied to her.

By the end of the class, Kit was brimming with enthusiasm for her chosen major. Professor Wentworth was engaging and knowledgeable and she knew he'd manage to keep the class interesting.

Stepping into the corridor, Kit noticed Francie and Charlotte lurking outside the door. From their excited expressions, Kit knew that they'd heard about the skeleton in her closet…er, floorboards. Another point for the Westdale gossip mill.

"Is it true?" Francie asked, her almond-shaped eyes morphing into walnuts.

Kit pursed her lips and nodded.

"This is why you should always outsource your renovations," Francie said solemnly.

"Tell us everything," Charlotte insisted.

Kit glanced over her shoulder, not wanting to be overheard. "Let's go to Butter Beans where we can hide in a corner. I don't think I'm supposed to be blabbing about everything I know."

Butter Beans was busier than usual and Kit realized it was because classes were now in full swing. She'd need to ask Sam when the best times were to come. She didn't want to battle for a seat every time she stopped by.

They waited in the long line for drinks and chatted about school until they could sit down and quietly discuss Kit's discovery.

"Which other classes do you have?" Kit asked. It would be nice to know if they shared any other classes.

Charlotte pulled out a color-coded, laminated schedule.

"What is that?" Kit asked, craning her neck to see.

"It's my schedule," Charlotte replied, waving it at her.

Kit stopped Charlotte's hand from moving so she could get a closer look. "Why does it remind you to brush your teeth at seven in the morning?"

Charlotte tucked away the schedule. "I have organizational issues."

"And working memory, too," Francie added. "It's all part of her dyspraxia. Remember? I mentioned it the other day at the fountain."

"But what if you lose the laminated card?" Kit asked. "Will you forget to brush your teeth?"

"Hopefully not. I've gotten pretty good with the basics." Charlotte held up her phone. "Anyway, the card is a backup. I also have reminder alarms on my phone."

"The card is in case she drops her phone into a toilet or a fountain," Francie added.

"Both of which have happened," Charlotte added. "Or I just lose the phone completely."

"How do you cope?" Kit asked. As an actress, she'd relied so heavily on her memory and physical skills that she couldn't imagine functioning with Charlotte's condition.

"Daniel Radcliffe has dyspraxia," Charlotte said, as though she knew what Kit was thinking. "He managed okay as Harry Potter."

"He sure did," Kit agreed.

They finally got their turn at the counter and placed their order. Sam wasn't working this shift so at least Kit didn't need to field any questions about whether Orson Welles was, indeed, the greatest filmmaker of all time. As if she'd worked with him personally.

There were no seats available by the time they retrieved their drinks so they hovered between a few tables, sipping their drinks.

"I'm surprised no one notices you," Charlotte whispered. "You're a pretty big name in Westdale."

Kit shrugged. "I don't think Westdale viewers featured into the demographics for Fool's Gold."

Francie lit up. "That's not what she means." She cleared her throat and increased her volume. "Oh my goodness, I had no idea you were the daughter of Heloise Winthrop Wilder. I do apologize for my ignorance. Your mother is an inspiration to us all."

A middle-aged man glanced up from his newspaper and Kit noticed that he was reading the Westdale Gazette. She didn't think anyone read the actual paper anymore.

"Would you ladies like this table?" he offered. "I'm finished with it."

Francie placed a grateful hand on her chest. "That is so sweet. Thank you." She winked at Kit as he gathered his belongings and vacated the premises.

They sat down at the available table and Kit grumbled under her breath.

"What's the matter?" Charlotte asked.

"This is what my life is going to be, isn't it?" Kit moaned. "No matter what I do for myself, as long as I'm in Westdale, the only thing that matters is who my mother is."

Charlotte shook her blond ponytail. "No, I'm pretty sure who your father is matters, too."

Kit groaned again and covered her face with her hands. "Between the dead guy in my house and the wide sphere of influence held by my mother, I'm regretting the decision to move back here."

Francie and Charlotte exchanged looks. "Well, we're not sorry," Francie said. "We're happy to have you here and not because of your mother or father."

"That's only because your families are on par with the Winthrops and Wilders," Kit pointed out. "You don't need Heloise's favor."

"Yes, but we sure don't want to be out of her favor either," Francie said.

Kit understood the sentiment all too well.

"So tell us about the murder," Charlotte urged. "Who was it?"

Kit told them about Ernie and the relevant neighborhood gossip.

"Are you scared to sleep there?" Charlotte asked. "I mean, what if the murderer comes back?"

"Why would the murderer come back?" Kit asked. "The victim is clearly dead."

Charlotte lowered her voice. "What about the victim's ghost?"

Francie gave her friend's leg a gentle smack. "Charlotte Tilton, don't talk like that. You'll scare Kit straight back into Greyabbey."

"No she won't," Kit said. "Believe me, my mother is far scarier than any dead man's ghost could ever be. Anyway, I'm already back at Greyabbey until the police finish checking the house over for evidence. I doubt they'll find any, though. Ernie's stuff was moved out by the bank ages ago and I tore up the carpet that had been put down to conceal the floorboards."

"Somebody went to a lot of trouble to hide the body," Francie said.

"And they would've gotten away with it, too, if I hadn't decided to renovate."

"So where's Ernie's stuff now?" Charlotte asked.

"In a storage unit," Kit replied. "The police are investigating there, too."

Francie rubbed her hands together excitedly. "This is so exciting. A real crime in Westdale."

"My father wants to know why the paper hasn't reported it," Charlotte said. "He's so ill most of the time, all he does is read. I think he was hoping to read about something more salacious than the Pilgrim Society tea party."

Kit's brow wrinkled. "I don't know. I guess I'll need to ask Crispin. It does seem odd."

In fact, everything about this murder seemed odd. Kit hoped the police figured it out soon because she wouldn't be

55

able to fully embrace her new life until she was back in her new home.

Chapter Four

After her chat with the girls in Butter Beans, Kit decided to swing by the house and check on police progress. She figured her presence might remind them that someone actually lived in the house besides a skeleton. She opened the front door and stepped into the middle of a heated argument between Chief Riley and Romeo.

"Who loses a body?" Romeo demanded, standing perilously close to Chief Riley. The chief was wider but Romeo had the height advantage.

"Technically, it was no longer a body," Chief Riley said. "And I don't know what the hell happened. My boys told me they delivered the remains to West Chester."

"To the M.E.'s office or to a random guy in the parking lot?" Romeo shot back. "Or do they not know the difference?"

"They're good cops," Chief Riley insisted. "The bones will turn up." Chief Riley's voice shot up an octave. His face was beet red and Kit worried that he'd suffer cardiac arrest in her house. The last thing she needed was another dead man in her living room.

"Now how are we going to establish cause of death?" Romeo muttered.

"Gentlemen, I can see there's an issue," Kit said, placing herself between them. "How about we take a second to breathe?"

"Westdale cops are a joke," Romeo continued. "How hard is it to transport something from Point A to Point B? We would've been better off calling the UPS guy to take care of it."

Chief Riley puffed out his chest. "I'll be on the phone with Sheriff Jackson in two minutes if you keep this up."

"Good. She'll tan your hide for me." Romeo took a step back and raked his hands through his thick hair. "I shouldn't have agreed to let your guys take care of it. I had the forensics team on site."

Chief Riley's shoulder relaxed and he adopted a calmer tone. "It was a big deal to them. County handles all the big cases. They just wanted to feel like a part of the action for a change."

Romeo pointed a finger at the chief. "You need to fix this and fast. I don't want to be the whipping boy for Westdale's screw-ups."

"I'll do my best," he promised before high-tailing it off the premises.

"Well, that was awkward timing," Kit said. "I take it there was a bit of a snafu with Mr. Ludwig's remains."

Romeo paced the living room floor. "Tweedle Dee and Tweedle Numbnut say they delivered the remains but the M.E.'s office doesn't have them."

Kit thought Jamison and Harley were nice enough guys, but she wasn't about to vouch for their competence. "They're still learning," she said.

"I'd rather they learn about how to write a parking ticket and stay out of my murder investigation."

Kit resisted the urge to wrap a comforting arm around his broad shoulders. "The chief is right, Romeo. This is a murder in affluent Westdale, their turf. People like to flex their power muscles here. Harley and Jamison don't want the Pilgrim Society coming down on them for not solving the murder right away. If they upset the wrong people, they'd get fired."

"Fine. Maybe I'll let them join my team over at the storage unit," he grumbled.

"The one with Ernie's things?"

Romeo nodded. "My guys have been searching for any evidence they can find."

"Like a murder weapon?"

"Anything. Evidence of a struggle. Blood stains. You name it, but that unit is chock full of junk."

"That might be the thing to keep the Tweedle twins busy then."

"So explain this Pilgrim Society to me," Romeo said, resting an elbow on the wooden mantle. "Why do people think they're better than everyone else because of sharing a little DNA with someone hundreds of years before their time?"

"Why are you so proud of your Italian heritage?" Kit shot back. "It's the same idea."

"Somebody's defensive considering the way she rolls her eyes at the mere mention of Mayflower or Pilgrims."

He was right. Kit was being defensive, but the Mayflower descendants were her people, like it or not. She'd defend them to anyone, despite her personal feelings on the subject. That was just her way.

"These social events are an excuse to parade around and feel superior," Kit explained. "Like your Columbus Day parade or whatever it is your people do."

Romeo suppressed a grin. "My people tend to talk loudly and gesticulate."

"My people talk softly, mainly idle gossip or, if it's a pissing contest, about the wings of hospitals that have recently been named for them."

Romeo inclined his head. "They do gossip at these meetings, don't they?"

"Of course. It's in the by-laws."

"Are you allowed to bring a guest?" he asked, his dark brown eyes glimmering in the subdued light.

"Is this your way of angling for a date?" Kit asked.

"It's my way of angling for inside information," he replied.

Kit felt like a complete idiot. Of course that was the reason. As usual, his interest in her had nothing to do with the pleasure of her company.

"Well, I'm sorry to tell you that attendance is by invitation only and you need to be a bonafide descendant."

"So even if I had proof of a Pilgrim ancestor, I'd still need a special invitation?"

Kit shrugged. "It's a selective group, what can I tell you?"

He leaned closer, his soft breath warming the curve of her neck. "You can tell me if anyone discusses the bones found in your house. Anyone who sounds like they know more than they should."

Kit's eyes widened. "I was kidding. No way am I going to one of these meetings. I hate all of that. I left here to get away from it."

"But now you're back," Romeo said pointedly. "And I assume you want to move back into your new house as quickly as possible, right?"

Kit's hands flew to her hips. "Are you blackmailing me, Officer Moretti?"

"It's Detective," he corrected her. "And it's not blackmail. I'm simply suggesting that the sooner we close this case, the sooner you get to put a few beautifully manicured lawns between you and your Mayflower Mama."

Kit crossed her arms like a petulant child. One meeting. What harm could it do?

"Fine, I'll go," she huffed.

"Great," he said. "Call me when it finishes and I'll meet you at Provincetown Pancakes for a debrief."

Kit raised her eyebrows. "Your usual hangout?"

He winked. "Who doesn't love a good short stack?"

Kit tried not to think about the amount of carbs and sugar involved in any dish at Provincetown Pancakes. She'd order a peppermint tea and then be on her way.

"Oh and Kit," he called as she turned to leave. "Turn off the location feature on your Instagram and Twitter accounts. It's fine to offer a running commentary at the nail salon, but we don't need the world knowing about our rendezvous."

Kit's cheeks flamed and she stalked off, embarrassed on multiple fronts. Romeo Moretti was checking her out on Twitter and Instagram. Maybe his interest was more personal than professional. It was hard to tell at this point, but she had to admit that no matter what his agenda was — she really liked hearing him say the word 'rendezvous.'

Kit went to the meeting separately from her mother so that she could sneak off to Provincetown Pancakes afterward without arousing suspicion. Besides, Heloise never walked anywhere. Why walk when you had a driver at your disposal?

By the time Kit arrived at the historic Weston Inn in Liberty Square, her mother was already holding court. Easy to do when you were the leader of the pack.

"Katherine, darling, you found us," her mother called, extending the hand unburdened by a cocktail.

"It's the Weston Inn, not the lost city of Atlantis."

Heloise laughed, a deep, throaty laugh that was infectious to the two people flanking her. Kit recognized one of the women, but couldn't remember her name.

"Katherine, you remember Cecilia Musgrove," Heloise said, nodding to her left, "and this exquisite young woman on my right is Rebecca Tilton. Her father, John, usually attends but the poor dear has been unwell." She cast a sympathetic look in Rebecca's direction.

"Musgrove," Kit repeated. "Is your daughter Francie?"

Cecelia's thin lips stretched into a smile that showed off her pearl white, perfectly rectangular teeth.

"Why, yes. Francie is my youngest. Have you met her?"

"She's in my class at Westdale."

"Indeed," Cecelia replied and made no further comment.

Kit wondered how often Cecelia engaged in meaningful conversation with her daughter. She suspected not very often at all. Kit sensed that Cecelia Musgrove was the type of woman too busy with charity events and a social calendar to pay any attention to a menial distraction like a spare child. Looking at her now, the only part of Cecelia that reminded Kit of Francie was the blond hair, and Kit suspected that only Francie's was authentic.

"Then you must know my sister, too," Rebecca interjected. "Charlotte and Francie are inseparable."

Kit's face lit up. "Of course, Charlotte Tilton. I didn't realize they were both members here."

"Francie is not a member," Cecelia scoffed. "You've been away too long, Katherine. Membership is only offered to the eldest."

Rebecca's gaze dropped to her black Stuart Weitzman heels, clearly uncomfortable with the old-fashioned prejudice. With that attitude, it was surprising that they'd found it prudent to open membership to women. It seemed to Kit that descendants should just be grateful that they made it this far, rather than erecting barriers within their own group.

"Rebecca, would you be so kind as to show my daughter where the drinks are located?" Heloise asked sweetly. "Her hand looks sad and lonely."

"A hand is not a hand without a drink to hold," Kit quoted. One of her mother's many nonsensical expressions.

Rebecca looped her arm through Kit's and guided her to the back of the room where the bar was located. "We heard about your unfortunate discovery," Rebecca said in a low voice.

"The police seem to be keeping it pretty quiet," Kit remarked. "How did you find out?"

glanced nervously behind them. "Francie
⁚ilia Musgrove speaking to Chief Riley and told
__arlotte told Father and me."

"I wondered how they knew," Kit said. "Why was Chief Riley speaking to Cecelia about it?"

Rebecca shrugged. "I couldn't say. Cecelia is awfully powerful, you know. Not quite your mother's level, mind you, but not much escapes her notice."

"I got your vodka tonic right here," a shrill voice said.

Kit spun around to find herself face-to-face with the male version of herself. "Crispin," she said happily, throwing her arms his neck. Even though they were first cousins, people had often mistaken them for brother and sister as children. They both had the same blue eyes with gold flecks and chestnut-colored hair. His younger sister, Arabella, favored her mother whereas Crispin and Kit shared Winthrop physical traits.

He handed her the vodka tonic. "Your mother said you might show. I bet Huntley twenty dollars that you wouldn't."

"It was a last minute decision," Kit admitted, not wanting to say anything else on the subject.

Crispin owned the local newspaper, the Westdale Gazette. As a general rule, he was the last person she'd confide in. Not to mention he'd been a first class tattletale from the time he could talk. He'd gotten Kit into trouble on many occasions, especially during their teen years. They hadn't even attended the same high school — she'd gone to the Shiphay School, an all girls' school, and he'd gone the neighboring all boys' school — yet he'd still managed to sink her sneaky ship whenever the opportunity had presented itself. Crispin Winthrop was a world-class snitch. Still, she loved him like a brother.

"Shall I get you another drink?" Crispin asked Rebecca, nodding toward her empty glass.

"Just lemonade for me," she said. "I'm driving and I need to be on my toes for my father."

They joined Crispin at the bar so he could order the lemonade. "My mother said that your father is ill," Kit remarked.

Rebecca nodded. "Cancer. It hit him hard and fast. I've taken a semester off from medical school to spend time with him."

"What about your mother?" Kit asked.

"Mother?" Rebecca blinked. "She died when I was ten. Father remarried last year, but, with my medical training, we felt that I was better suited to look after him."

"I'm sorry to hear that." Kit could tell there was more to the story than Rebecca was admitting, but she didn't push the issue. Rebecca was obviously a devoted and loving daughter, just what her father needed.

Kit surveyed the room, trying to decide how to dig for information without offering too much of her own. This would prove more difficult than she'd anticipated. In that moment, she realized that she never had to think as Ellie Gold, her thoughts and actions had been dictated for her, not unlike her childhood.

Her gaze wandered back to Cecilia Musgrove. She'd had a private conversation with Chief Riley on the subject. Maybe there was a reason for that.

"Shall we rejoin Cecelia and my mother?" Kit proposed.

Crispin eyed her curiously. "You are voluntarily returning to your mother's side?" He grabbed her drink and took a sip. "Nope, no drugs in there."

"Hey, that reminds me. Why haven't you reported on the skeleton in my house? I would think that's big news in Westdale."

Crispin swilled his own drink. "And tip people off that you're living alone on Thornhill Road?" he queried. "I love you too much to do that to you. You'd have paparazzi and weirdos pitching tents on your front lawn in no time. The neighbors will hate you."

Despite the sweetness of the sentiment, Kit didn't buy it for a second. For one thing, the Crispin she knew would rat her out in a heartbeat if it meant a good story. The real tipoff, however, was Crispin's demeanor. His eyes were focused anywhere except on her. In her experience with the Winthrop branch of her family, that meant he was lying. But why?

Kit immediately spotted Romeo in a booth at the back of the room. He didn't glance up from the menu until she slid into the seat across from him. He was dressed in what she assumed was part of his summer casual collection — neatly pressed khakis and a red shirt.

"Where's your suit?" she asked. "I hardly recognized you in costume."

"I'm trying to blend," he said.

"People in Westdale wear suits," Kit objected.

"Not in the pancake joint at ten o'clock at night," he replied. He handed her a menu. "So what'd you find out?"

"My mother can drink anybody under the table. Cranberry is the new raspberry. I have a high tolerance for alcohol but a low tolerance for entitled snobs."

Romeo didn't bother to hide his amusement. "And what did you find out that is relevant to the investigation?"

A server appeared beside Kit, ready to take their order. She did a double take when she looked at Kit. "Omigod, you're her."

"I am often accused of being her," Kit said.

"Can I have your autograph?"

Kit smiled. "For a short stack with a side of blueberries, sure." She hadn't intended to splurge on calories tonight, but three vodka tonics at the Weston Inn had kickstarted her appetite.

"And you, sir?" the server asked Romeo.

"The Divine Sampler," he said, handing her both menus.

"Anything to drink?" the server asked.

"A large water for me," Kit said. Her mouth already felt full of cotton.

"Coffee, please," Romeo added.

The server practically skipped back to the kitchen. Kit found it strange that people wanted her autograph. She hadn't become an actress in order to be famous. That was simply an unwelcome by-product. After a few years, though, she'd gotten used to the attention.

"Coffee at ten o'clock?" Kit chided him. "You'll never get to sleep."

"Who said I'm going to sleep soon?" he asked.

Kit cleared her throat. Maybe Romeo had a girlfriend. A girlfriend who liked him in summer casualwear and didn't mind him sharing pancakes with a former television star.

"Okay, so I'll tell you what I learned tonight," she said. "I'm not sure if any of it is helpful, but I won't prejudge."

"Unlike your people."

"Unlike my people." She drew in a breath. "My cousin said he hasn't run the story about the murder because he doesn't want crazy stalkers at my house."

"Sounds reasonable."

"He's lying. I love Crispin, but he cheats at tennis and gin rummy and I have no doubt that there's another reason."

Romeo absorbed this nugget of information. "Anything else?"

"Cecilia Musgrove has been chatting with our beloved Chief Riley about the case."

"And?"

"And I don't know. It's sketchy."

"Sketchy? Did she know Ernie?"

Kit shook her head. "Don't think so. She's way too high in the pecking order to tolerate someone like him. She's a taller, icier version of my mother." She shivered at the thought.

"Okay, I'll drop in on Cecilia tomorrow afternoon. See what I can find out."

"You should do morning or afternoon," Kit advised. "She mentioned attending a fundraiser in Bryn Mawr tomorrow afternoon."

"I can't do morning," Romeo said.

"Sleeping in after your all-nighter?" Kit teased.

Romeo glanced at her quizzically. "No, I'm doing Adopt-a-Cop at a school in Philly."

Kit's eyes widened. "Do tell."

"You don't know about Adopt-a-Cop?" he queried. When she shook her head, he explained, "It's a program where we go into schools and talk to kids about self-esteem and how important it is to like yourself."

She snorted. The image of Romeo in an elementary school talking to kids about liking himself delighted Kit to no end.

"Why is that funny?" Romeo asked, not amused.

"It's not," Kit said, suppressing a smile. "It's adorable."

Romeo scowled. "It's not adorable. I talk about other things, too. I go to the same school every month during the school year. The first month is always self-esteem. Next month is drug safety." He gave her a pointed look. "It's serious police business. Definitely not adorable."

The server brought their drinks and promptly returned to the kitchen for their plates.

Kit was fascinated by this. Her school had offered no interaction with the police department. Then again, if someone like Romeo had shown up at her school, he'd have had twenty smitten girls offering their rapt attention...and their phone numbers.

The server returned with their meals and set the plates down. "Enjoy," she said before scuttling off.

"And you go every month?" Kit asked.

He nodded, sipping his coffee. "I talk about home safety, learning how to say no. Lots of stuff kids are exposed to. It's important to help kids feel safe talking to cops. A lot of neighborhoods see cops as the enemy." He glanced around the sleepy Provincetown Pancakes. "Even a place like Westdale."

Kit chuckled. "We're hardly the inner city."

Romeo's expression turned serious. "No, but you both build your same walls to keep outsiders out."

"Not so much keep people out as keep them in their proper places," Kit said.

"You're all white, wealthy and descended from Pilgrims. Why bother with assigned places?"

"Oh ye of little Westdale knowledge. There's a pecking order even among the descendants," Kit explained. "The Allertons were considered the saints. They were the religious contingency on board the Mayflower. Their descendants look down upon the Mullins descendants because Mullins was a mere merchant. Not a saint but a stranger. All of them look down upon the Doty descendants because Edward Doty had been not only a servant, but a servant to one of the merchants." Kit clucked her tongue. "For shame."

Romeo chuckled. "Let me guess. You're an Allerton descendant."

"I confess," she said. "I'm a saint."

"And yet you wanted to give up your social status here in favor of playing somebody's busty sidekick?"

Kit was both annoyed and elated by his statement. Annoyed because she was the star, not the sidekick. Elated because it meant that he'd checked out the show since their last meeting. And he thought she was busty. Was that a plus? She wasn't sure.

"The show was called Fool's Gold," she remarked. "I played Ellie Gold. Charlie Owen played my sidekick." Of course, now he was the star, even though they hadn't bothered to change the name of the show.

Romeo arched an eyebrow. "Somebody's defensive."

70

"I'm not defensive," Kit argued and heard the shrill sound of her own voice. She picked up her glass of water and chugged it in an effort to remain calm.

"Okay, relax," Romeo said, holding up a hand. "So do you think the murder might have something to do with Ernie not knowing his place? Where was he in the pecking order?"

Kit shook her head. "He wasn't in the Pilgrim Society. Not everyone in Westdale is a descendant."

"I thought maybe it was a residency requirement," Romeo joked. "Everyone else has to live in Eastdale."

Eastdale was the neighboring town across the Lenapehoking River. In Westdale, it was known as the 'wrong' side of the tracks, even though it was an upper middle class town with a desirable rail connection to Philadelphia.

"Eastdale? Bite your tongue, Detective," Kit said. "Anyway, I'd be surprised if his death had anything to do with the society. They're more interested in murder mystery fundraisers than actual murder."

Kit glanced down at Romeo's empty plate and realized that he'd managed to inhale his entire meal without her noticing. She still had two small pancakes left on her plate. He had an appetite, she'd say that for him. Somehow, it made him seem more appealing.

Romeo wiped his mouth with his cloth napkin. "I think it's commendable...what you're doing," he said.

"What am I doing?" she asked. "You mean helping with the investigation? That's for purely selfish reasons, you know that."

He inclined his head. "That's not what I'm talking about. I mean dusting yourself off after a very public fall and coming back to Westdale. Going to college. Not everyone would have made the smart decision."

"The jury's still out on whether it's a smart decision," Kit said, "but thanks."

Chapter Five

Kit drove her car across the bridge to Eastdale where Ricco's Auto Repair was located. Although the residents of Westdale owned cars that needed servicing, they wouldn't dream of allowing an auto repair shop to operate within its precious town borders. Like the train station and Dunkin' Donuts, auto repair shops were relegated to the other side of the Lenapehoking River.

Since Kit needed to have the car inspected within ten days of registration, she decided to nip it in the bud and do it right away. She'd ask the guy to affix the new Pennsylvania license plates as well. Two tasks, one handy man.

The mechanic's eyes sparkled at the sight of Kit's red Corvette Stingray pulling in to the shop. Kit was fully aware that the car was fancier than she was. A flashy car, however, was a requirement in Los Angeles. Between the valets and the paparazzi, Kit's car needed to be at least as eye-catching as she was.

"What a beauty," he said, punctuated by a whistle.

"Thanks. I thought about selling it when I moved back and getting something more...Westdale, but I can't bear to part with Betsy."

"You named a car like this Betsy?" he queried, wiping his greasy hands on a cloth. "No, no. This car is more of a Bolt or a Flash."

"You're giving my car superhero names," Kit remarked. "She's not that kind of car."

"Well, she should be." He eyed Kit. "You live in Westdale, you said?"

"Just moved back to start college."

He touched the hood of the car affectionately. "It's nice over there. I do a lot of work for Westdale folks. They're not as snooty as everybody makes them out to be."

"I highly doubt that." Kit leaned against the car, wondering if he'd dig himself any deeper.

The mechanic held up his hands. "No, seriously. My favorite customer in the whole world is in Westdale. She's batty as hell, but I have a soft spot for her. She's named after my favorite superhero."

"Would that be Bolt or Flash?" Kit teased.

"Thor," he replied.

Kit balked. "Thor? Do you mean Thora Breckenridge?"

The mechanic broke into a wide grin. "You know her, huh? She's a real hoot, right?"

"She's my neighbor. I moved into the empty house next door."

The mechanic clapped his hands gleefully. "So she finally managed to get rid of the jackass with the motor home?"

"You know about Ernie?" Kit asked. Thora certainly was chatty with her mechanic.

"Know about him? I almost got myself arrested because of him."

Kit's radar pinged wildly. "Really? What happened?" Clearly, news of Ernie's demise hadn't reached Eastdale or she doubted the mechanic would be so forthcoming.

"Poor Thora. She came in here one day all upset because her roses were dying. Ever since he'd parked that behemoth in his driveway, her flowers couldn't get enough light. She'd complained to me before, but this time she actually cried." He paused, remembering. "It was like watching my mima cry. I couldn't handle it so I asked her if there was anything I could do."

"And what did she say?"

"She asked if there was any way I could get rid of the motor home with my tow truck."

Kit laughed. "She wanted you to brazenly drive up, hook up your tow truck and pull his motor home away? To where?"

The mechanic shook his head. "She wanted me to switch out the plates. You know, really get rid of it." He cleared his throat, not wanting to acknowledge that his skills extended beyond the letter of the law.

"That was a big request."

"I came at night. From what Thora said, most of the folks on that street are pretty old. I figured they'd all be asleep by then or too blind and deaf to hear my truck." He gave Kit an appraising look. "That was before you moved in, of course."

"Of course."

"Anyways, Ernie wasn't as old and feeble as I thought. He apparently heard the truck and came barreling out of the house, shouting obscenities at me."

Kit covered her mouth. "Did he call the police?"

"He threatened to. I swore it was an honest mistake and that someone had called me with his address, pretending to need a tow."

"Quick thinking," Kit said.

The mechanic shrugged. "Not my first botched job." He glanced quickly at Kit's expensive car. "I mean…"

Kit patted his arm reassuringly. "I know what you mean. I trust you with Betsy." She searched his shirt for a nametag. "What's your name?"

"Chris."

"I trust you, Chris. Anyone who goes to bat for an elderly woman is okay in my book."

Chris grinned. "Gotta love Thora. She's so crazy."

Crazy like a fox, Kit thought and handed Chris the keys.

Kit's thoughts were still on crafty Thora Breckenridge during dinner at Greyabbey with her mother and Huntley.

"I ran into Margaret Toulouse yesterday at the hair salon," her mother began and Kit's insides twisted. She knew what was coming next. "Imagine my surprise when she said that you haven't been attending her classes."

"I'm not attending them because I haven't signed up for her class," Kit said.

Margaret Toulouse was an art history professor at Westdale College. She and Heloise had attended Princeton together and Margaret had been a guest at Greyabbey on multiple occasions over the years.

Heloise appeared genuinely shocked. "But you enrolled in Westdale," she said.

"I did." Kit speared a piece of asparagus. "But I'm not majoring in art history. I decided to major in psychology." She watched her mother closely for signs of heart failure.

Heloise stiffened, then reached for her water goblet. "Good God, Diane. When is Jesus arriving to turn this into wine?"

"I can bring dessert out if you're ready," Diane offered.

"What does dessert have to do with anything?" Heloise demanded.

Diane lowered her voice. "It's plum gin sorbet. I found a special recipe for you."

Gin and sorbet in one recipe? Heloise lit up like a Christmas tree. "That's the best thing I've ever heard." She glanced sharply at Kit. "Hurry up and finish so Diane can bring out dessert."

Never in her life had Kit been asked to hurry and finish her dinner so that dessert could be served. Heloise was a stickler for table manners. At least she had been when Kit's father was still alive. It seemed that they had both changed since his untimely death.

Heloise said nothing further on the topic of Kit's major. Kit knew better than to think the issue was resolved. Her mother was simply tucking the disclosure away for later derision.

"Who is the dark, swarthy man you've been seen around town with?" Heloise asked.

Huntley shot Kit an inquisitive look. It seemed they were both interested in the answer to her question.

"By dark and swarthy, do you mean the olive-skinned gentleman of Italian descent?"

Heloise narrowed her eyes. "I suppose I do."

"He's the lead detective in the murder investigation," Kit said.

"And why are you spending time with him?" Heloise pressed.

"I'm not spending time with him in that way," Kit said, although she wished she was. "I'm helping him with the investigation so I can go back to my house."

"Oh," Heloise said quietly. "Well, Crispin said his friend..." She looked to Huntley for help. "What's his name again, darling?"

"Frederick Breedlove."

"Mr. Breedlove is dying to meet you now that you're back. Maybe doubles at the club with Crispin and Arabella?"

"No," Kit objected, both on principle and the fact that the guy's name was Breedlove. "Not until I'm settled. I just started classes and I'm making friends. I don't want to get sidetracked."

"Sidetracked?" Heloise echoed. "Meeting your future husband is not getting sidetracked." She enunciated the latter part of the sentence, emphasizing her dismay.

"If you think I'm going to become Kit Breedlove, you're more delusional than I thought."

"Oh Katherine, don't be so dramatic," her mother scolded. "You get that from Grandma Josephine."

"You're the one who was intent on having me enroll in Westdale College," Kit said. "Why bother if you want me to focus on snagging a husband?"

"A degree is important," Heloise acknowledged, "but a husband is more important."

Kit rolled her eyes. "Excuse me while I eject myself from the time machine I seem to be trapped in."

"It's true," Heloise insisted. "And what on earth do you intend to do with a degree in psychology?"

"I haven't decided yet. Maybe become a psychologist." She watched in awe as her mother spoon fed a dollop of plum gin sorbet to Hermes, the Giant Schnauzer. "God knows I have plenty of experience with crazy people."

Kit made a show of weeding her front garden in the hope that Thora would emerge from her house. Just because she couldn't live in the house didn't mean she couldn't care for the exterior. The house had been unloved long enough.

Kit kneeled in the hot sun, sweat dripping down her chest. She knew it would be easier to go knock on the door and ask about Chris the mechanic, but she wanted their exchange to be subtle so she could gauge Thora's reaction. That's what Ellie Gold would do.

In episode five, season one of Fool's Gold, Ellie dealt with an elderly woman in a nursing home who the police believed had witnessed a crime. They thought that the elderly woman didn't want to admit what she'd seen because she was afraid. It turned out that she didn't want to admit her presence at the crime scene because she was actually the culprit. Ellie's trick in that episode had been to gain the woman's trust. No one in her family ever came to visit her in the nursing home and she craved human interaction so she began to look forward to Ellie's visits, even if they were crime-related.

Kit stole a look at the quiet house next door. Maybe Thora was out, although her car was in the driveway.

Kit yanked another root from the ground and yelped when dirt from the roots flew into her eyes.

"That's not a weed," a shaky voice called. Kit watched as Thora ambled her way across the front lawn. "Are you trying to give an old woman a stroke pulling out your asters?"

Well, there was nothing wrong with Thora's eyesight, that was certain.

"Those are flowers?" Kit asked, incredulous. "I thought I was being a diligent gardener."

"What are you even doing here?" Thora asked. "Have the police finished the investigation?"

"Not to my knowledge," Kit replied, wondering just how desperately Thora wanted to know.

Thora put a hand on her replacement hip, scrutinizing Kit's abysmal handiwork. "How much do you know about gardening?"

Kit shielded her eyes, gazing up at Thora. "Well, we have beautiful gardens at Greyabbey."

"And you tended to these gardens yourself?" Thora quizzed her, knowing perfectly well that the Winthrop Wilders had staff for everything.

"I watched," Kit said, then added meekly, "sometimes."

Thora studied the flowerbed with a critical eye. "These are daisies. You've heard of daisies, haven't you? They need partial sun and plenty of water. Those are tomato plants. They shouldn't even be in this bed. It's an offense against nature." She huffed in disgust. "Ernie Ludwig had no sense of decency."

"You are dead serious about gardens," Kit said and winced when she realized she'd used the word 'dead.'

"The Westdale garden competition is once a year." She held up her index finger in Kit's face. "Once. I won every year until…"

"Until?" Kit prompted. "Ernie's motor home?"

Thora nodded and adjusted the hem of her shirt. "Now I'm back in business, thank goodness." She rubbed her hands together excitedly. "I'm sure to win this year."

"When do they judge?"

"September. You'll see how gorgeous my garden looks by then."

"Unless I buy that motor home I had my eye on," Kit joked. The steely look in Thora's eye made Kit nervous. "Just kidding," she said feebly. Kit decided to hold off on asking about Chris the mechanic. Somehow, it didn't seem like the right moment anymore.

After Thora returned to her house for a nap, Kit carried on attacking her garden in light of Thora's helpful tips. Murderer or not, the older woman knew her way around a flowerbed.

An unfamiliar black car pulled into the driveway next door and Kit recognized Romeo's profile at the wheel. Quickly, she smoothed her hair and wiped the dirt from her face with the bottom of her shirt. She looked like a hot mess, but there was nowhere to hide.

"Didn't expect to see you here," Romeo said, sauntering over to where she knelt.

"I could say the same to you." She flashed him a megawatt smile, hoping her Julia Roberts-style mouth distracted him from the rest of her grungy self.

"I'm interviewing Peregrine Monroe."

"By yourself?" Kit asked.

"I'm a pretty big boy," Romeo replied with amusement.

"It isn't that," she said, dusting off her knees as she stood. "Let me come with you. It'll give you an air of legitimacy."

"I think the badge and gun help with legitimacy," he said, showing her his concealed weapon.

Kit rolled her eyes. "You really don't get it. You're an outsider."

"Some think you are, too," he commented.

"Fair enough, but I'm better than no one."

"Older women love me."

"Not this one. Peregrine Monroe is not going to take a shine to you. Trust me."

Romeo studied her for a moment. "Kit, seriously…"

"How'd you do with Cecilia Musgrove?" she inquired. His dark eyes shifted to the flowers and Kit had her answer. "Big surprise there. My mother would eat you for lunch so you'd at least be an appetizer for Cecilia."

Romeo pulled a handkerchief from his suit pocket and handed it to Kit. "Okay, fine, but clean yourself up first. You can't go dripping sweat in the lady's house. Your DNA will be everywhere."

"Are you expecting another crime to be committed?" She swiped the handkerchief and wiped her face and the back of her neck. When she finished, she noticed that Romeo was staring at her.

"What?" she asked, touching her face. "Did I squish a mosquito or something?"

"No," Romeo said. "That was just much sexier than I thought it would be."

Kit blushed and tucked the handkerchief in her back pocket. "I'll wash it before I give it back."

He glanced appreciatively at her backside where the handkerchief protruded from her pocket. "First time in my life I ever wanted to be a handkerchief."

Kit yanked out the handkerchief and swatted his arm with it as they strode up to Peregrine's door. His knock was loud and firm. Kit wouldn't have been surprised if the entire block heard it.

The door opened and Peregrine eyed them warily. "Yes?"

"Ms. Monroe, we met before. I'd asked you a few questions about the last time you saw Ernie Ludwig."

"Do you need something, Detective? I'm afraid I'm rather busy."

"Packing for Sedona?" Romeo asked casually. "I think it'll be hotter than hell there now."

Kit tried to disguise her shock. Romeo knew about Sedona?

Peregrine opened the door stiffly. "Do come in. I suppose I can spare a few moments."

They stepped inside and she immediately offered them iced tea. Kit gratefully accepted. She was beyond parched from her gardening work.

"I'm glad to see you're sprucing up the front yard," Peregrine said, a note of approval in her voice. "It was in dire need of a green thumb."

"I don't know how green my thumb is," Kit confessed, "but Thora seems to have adopted me as her protégé."

"If that's true, then consider yourself lucky," Peregrine said. "The woman is a gardening marvel."

83

"Not like Ernie Ludwig, huh?" Romeo asked, turning the conversation toward the real reason for his visit.

"No, not at all like him," Peregrine said bitterly.

"You don't think it's odd that the minute we discover Ernie's body, you decide to move across the country?" Romeo asked.

"I can't help where my sister lives," Peregrine replied. Although her body was rigid, Kit knew she couldn't read anything into it. Rigid was Peregrine's natural state.

"But you can help when you decide to join her there," Romeo countered.

Peregrine set down her glass and met Romeo's assessing gaze. "What is your real question, Detective? Shall I call my lawyer?"

"No, no. No need to spend five hundred bucks. Save it for your new place. I'm just here to have a conversation," Romeo assured her. "That's all."

"All right then. Can I offer you any macaroons?"

"Ooh, from Biscuits?" Kit asked hopefully.

"Have you been there since you moved home?" Peregrine asked, standing to retrieve the signature duck egg blue box.

"No, thank you for reminding me they exist." Kit accepted a macaroon. Turned out that gardening was thirsty and hungry work.

Romeo waved off the macaroons. "I know it was a long time ago, but can you recall anything unusual around the time Ernie disappeared?" he asked.

"We've had this conversation already," Peregrine pointed out.

"I asked you to think about it," Romeo retorted. "Were there any strangers prowling around? Was Ernie behaving oddly?"

Peregrine looked thoughtful, although Kit doubted very much that Peregrine knew Ernie well enough to judge whether his actions had been out of character. Peregrine had more likely given her neighbor a wide berth.

"There was an unfamiliar car one day," she remarked. "Not long before Ernie went missing."

Romeo flipped open his notepad. "Can you describe the car?"

"White with an orange stripe on the side." She pursed her lips. "It wasn't a Westdale car."

"That you recognized," Romeo clarified.

"No, I mean it was not a Westdale car," she insisted. "No one here would dream of owning a car like that." Her lips curled and Romeo got the message. No muscle cars in Westdale.

"Any chance you caught the license plate number?" he asked.

"No, I'm afraid not."

"Did you get a look at the driver?"

"A man," she said. "He didn't even stop, that I noticed. He just drove slowly down the street and idled for a moment in front of Ernie's house."

"Are you a member of the Pilgrim Society?" Romeo asked, shifting gears.

Kit wasn't sure why society membership was relevant to the investigation.

"I was, once upon a time," Peregrine said.

"Not now?" Romeo prodded.

85

She gave a crisp shake of her head. "They seem to let in anyone these days."

Kit wasn't sure who 'anyone' was. It seemed to her that the restrictive membership policy was still firmly in place.

"How so?" Romeo asked.

"Well, they're not even requiring background checks on members. They may as well include descendants of the springer spaniel," she complained bitterly.

"There was a springer spaniel on board the ship," Kit explained softly.

"Ms. Monroe, when do you intend to join your sister in Sedona?" Romeo asked.

"I was planning to leave tomorrow," she said. "I'm waiting to list the house until the investigation is over."

"Well, I'd like to ask you to stick around," Romeo said. "Maybe reschedule your flight until the investigation is over, too."

Peregrine inhaled sharply. Clearly, she was not expecting this news. "But my sister's expecting me."

"I think it's best if you postpone," Romeo said. "In case we have more questions."

"But I've told you everything I know," Peregrine complained.

"I'm sorry, Ms. Monroe," Romeo said and Kit was impressed that he truly did look sorry. "It's standard procedure."

"For criminals," she objected. "I'm not a criminal."

Romeo offered her a sympathetic smile. "Even so, we'd like you to follow the procedure."

Peregrine raised her chin a fraction. "Fine, I'll show you out."

"I am sorry for the inconvenience," Romeo said in the doorway.

Peregrine managed a smile. "I do understand. And you're welcome any time, although I would prefer that you call ahead."

Once they were deposited on the front step, Kit turned to her companion. "Yeah, she really doesn't like you."

"What are you talking about?" he said. "I was a big hit. She offered me macaroons."

"If she liked you, she would have offered you Scotch and a cigar."

"But she just said I was welcome any time. You heard her. She even smiled."

"She was baring her teeth. Sheesh, don't they teach you anything in cop school?" Kit spoke quietly as she accompanied him back to his car. "I need to share new information with you."

Romeo leaned against the car door. "I'm listening."

Kit peered over his shoulder and noticed Phyllis in the living room window. "Unfortunately, so are the neighbors." Kit liked Phyllis and she didn't want the older woman to know she was about to rat out her best friend.

Romeo opened the passenger door and gestured her forward. "Step into my office."

Kit ducked inside. She knew this move would set neighborly tongues wagging, but it was better than being overheard.

Once Romeo pulled the car onto Keystone Road, Kit told him about Thora and Chris, the mechanic.

"Wait, why were you at the auto repair shop?" he asked. "You don't have a car."

"I do have a car. I had it shipped from L.A. and needed to have it inspected."

"So why wasn't it in your driveway?" he asked.

Nothing slipped past him. "It's parked at Greyabbey since that's where I'm forced to live against my will," she reminded him. "I like to walk around town as much as possible. I missed that in L.A."

"What kind of car?" Romeo asked.

Kit tapped his temple. "Turn off the male part of your brain. The type of car isn't relevant to this conversation. I'm trying to tell you something important about the case."

Romeo grinned. "There's plenty of time for that. What kind of car? I'll bet it's a flashy sports car. I'm pretty sure it's against the law to drive a piece of crap in the state of California."

"We do not have plenty of time," Kit argued. "It takes three minutes to drive around the block."

He raised an eyebrow. "Who says we're driving around the block?"

Kit glanced down at the state of her appearance. "Romeo, I've been sweating my keister off in the front yard. This is an unauthorized outing."

"I've seen you look worse. You don't seem too selective about your Instagram selfies."

"Gee, thanks." She smoothed her hair. "So where are we going?"

"To Eastdale. I'd like to have a word with the mechanic."

Kit hesitated. "You really just want to ask him what kind of car I have, don't you?"

Romeo shrugged good-naturedly. "It's a critical part of my investigation."

"I was wondering if it's possible..." Kit trailed off, not sure if she wanted to speculate. Chris seemed like a nice enough guy and she'd taken a shine to Thora.

"You're wondering if it's possible that a sweet lady like Thora and the helpful mechanic accidentally killed Ernie?"

Kit's eyes widened. "How did you know?"

Romeo chuckled. "I'm a detective, remember?"

"Well, what if Ernie came out when Chris was trying to take the motor home and, in an effort to stop him, Ernie ended up underneath it somehow? Could the weight of a motor home explain the condition of his chest? That would explain why the motor home is missing. It was evidence."

Romeo appeared to mull it over. "If we ever locate the runaway skeleton, I'll mention it to the medical examiner, but I would've thought we'd have seen broken bones if that had been the case."

Kit felt a wave of relief. She hated to implicate either one of them.

"It doesn't mean they weren't responsible, though," Romeo added and Kit's stomach tensed. "It could still have happened when Chris tried to tow the motor home. Just some other way."

"So they haven't found the skeleton yet, huh?"

Romeo tightened his grip on the wheel. "Evidence goes missing. That part's not unusual, but a whole intact skeleton?" He shook his head. "Something's off."

"Are you looking into it?" Kit asked.

"Not me personally." His mouth quirked. "My snitch is keeping me pretty busy running down leads."

They crossed the bridge into Eastdale and Kit took a moment to admire the picturesque boathouses on Mayflower Row. She'd spent a lot of time there in her youth and the sudden view of it flooded her with nostalgia.

"You missed it here more than you thought," Romeo observed.

Kit leaned her cheek against the window. "I never intended to come back."

"So why did you?"

"I didn't have much of a choice."

"There's always a choice," he replied.

After Romeo dropped her off at the front gate, Kit dragged herself up the pathway to Greyabbey and prayed that her mother was at the country club. She didn't feel like being lectured about her poor choice of majors or her poor choice of houses. Her poor choices in general.

There was no sign of Huntley or the dogs. Kit wondered if they were strolling the property. The estate was five acres in total so there was plenty of space for the dogs to roam freely without scaring the daylights out of any unsuspecting pedestrians.

Kit opened the front door quietly and crept up the stairs to her bedroom. Diane was probably in the kitchen preparing dinner. Kit thought she might pester the cook for a few recipes later. Now that she'd be eating most of her meals at her own house, whenever she was allowed back there, she decided that it would be handy to know how to prepare a few simple dishes. The internet was a good source for recipes, but Diane was a better one.

She dropped her backpack by the bed and felt a wave of exhaustion roll over her. She was bone tired and it baffled her. She'd worked ten hours days full of physical activity for years and never took so much as a ten-minute power nap. Why did sleepy Westdale have this effect on her?

The conversation with Chris had been brief. He seemed surprised to see Kit show up with a detective. She felt a little guilty about that part, but Romeo was polite and asked easy questions. He basically had Chris confirm what he'd told Kit. To Chris's obvious relief, Romeo didn't give the mechanic a hard time about what he'd intended to do with the motor home. He was more interested in solving the murder and it showed.

Kit sat down on the edge of her bed and checked the time. She could probably sneak in a nap before dinner and no one would know. Heloise preferred a later dinner and everyone was out now anyway.

She slipped off her sandals and inched her way to the top of the bed, sliding underneath the silk sheets. Her foot brushed against something at the base of the bed. Something that moved.

Kit moved her foot aside. "Which cat are you?" she asked the sheets. She tried to recall their names but failed miserably. "Miss Moneypenny?"

She glanced down at the movement under the sheets. The shape was all wrong for a cat. Something touched her leg and she bolted from the bed, throwing back the top sheet.

Kit screamed like she'd never screamed in her life, not even when she'd played Victim #2 in a low budget horror movie that she filmed during her first hiatus from Fool's Gold.

The long snake slithered its way out of her bed to the floor. Kit scrambled onto a nearby chair, which was useless because if the snake could get into her bed, it could get onto a chair. Her heart pounded and she gripped the back of the chair with both hands.

Her mother appeared in the doorway with a look of mild concern. "What would possibly make you scream like that, Katherine? Are you auditioning for the Westdale Plays and Players?"

"Watch out," Kit called. "There's a giant snake coming toward you."

Heloise bent down and scooped up the three-foot-long reptile. "Oh, have you not met Josephine?"

"Josephine?" Kit repeated incredulously. "You named the snake after Grandma? Wait, forget I asked. Of course you did."

Heloise planted a kiss on the snake's head. "I rescued her from an unworthy owner. She's a Western Gaboon viper and a little sweetheart."

"Aren't those venomous?" Kit asked, still atop the chair.

"Naturally," Heloise replied.

"It was in my bed," Kit said. "It could have bitten me."

"That's why we have vials of antivenin in the kitchen pantry."

Kit tried to steady her breathing. "Any other creatures lurking around here that I should know about? I mean, what happened to good, old-fashioned dogs, cats and horses?" Her mother had always shown an affinity for animals, but Huntley had failed to update Kit on these newer additions.

"Have you met Mr. Tumnus?" Heloise asked.

"Good God, please don't tell me you have a centaur."

Heloise wrapped Josephine around the back of her neck. "Don't be ridiculous. That Mr. Tumnus is a faun. Our Mr. Tumnus is a rat." She gave the doorframe a tap. "Dinner's at six-thirty."

Once she was gone, Kit dissolved into a heap on the chair. She couldn't stay at Greyabbey any longer than necessary. Not when there were vipers afoot. When had her mother become Dr. Doolittle? She had to solve this case and soon or she'd be checking into the asylum, although it seemed to her that she already had.

Chapter Six

Kit chose a blue shift dress to wear to the sports bar in Eastdale. Her look was casual yet classy, her preferred style. Between Westdale society functions and Hollywood galas, Kit wondered how she'd survived all these years. She blew out her hair and then ran the flattening iron through it to calm any frizz. High humidity wasn't doing her hair any favors.

She kept her makeup simple, applying a sheer coat of lip gloss and a touch of mascara. Her skin was smooth and unblemished so she didn't bother with any foundation. She'd sweat it away in an hour anyway if the bar was as full as she expected it to be.

Giving herself an approving nod in the mirror, she took a big-toothed selfie and uploaded it for her fans. If she ever had the chance to get back in the business, she'd grab it with both hands. In the meantime, she was determined not to lose her fan base.

There were immediate responses to her post and Kit felt pleased. Those Hollywood big shots didn't know what they'd thrown away. Kit Wilder brought viewers to their televisions. She brought ratings. Talk about fools.

On a whim, Kit decided to call Beatrice and check in. Maybe the ban had been lifted and Kit could return to her life. Dreamers gonna dream.

"Kit, doll, how's higher education?" Beatrice's voice was so loud, it tickled Kit's ear.

"Hi Beatrice. How's everything with you?"

"My lips are chapped from all the butt-kissing. Otherwise, I'm peachy. What's new in Pilgrimville?"

Kit smiled, despite herself. "It's fine. Listen, I spoke to Jordan the other day and he mentioned that Geoffrey Tinicum is directing an action film…"

Beatrice cut her off. "Not a snowball's chance in Texas, sweetheart. The company that's financing Geoffrey's pet project is owned by the same company as Fool's Gold."

"Oh," Kit said in a small voice. That was probably why Jordan had heard about it in the first place.

"Don't get me wrong, you'd be amazing in the role," Beatrice told her. "There's just no way Geoffrey would fight for you. It's his first time working with the company."

"And there are plenty of eager young actresses to choose from, I'm sure," Kit said, a sour taste in her mouth.

"I will keep gently pushing you," Beatrice said. "You know I'm happy to keep your name on people's lips, but for what it's worth, I think you're doing a smart thing."

"Moving back in with my mother like a loser?"

"That's temporary," Beatrice said dismissively. "You're building a new life for yourself with a firm foundation. You'd never have that here, no matter how successful you were. You'd always worry and wonder when the roles would dry up. When they did, what would you do at forty years old with no other work experience?"

Kit pressed her lips together. "Are you saying I should give up? Not try to make a comeback?"

"Of course not," Beatrice scolded her. "I would never say that. I want what you want. Not for nothing, but I only make money if you make a comeback."

"You're a patient woman then," Kit said.

"Damn right I am. Plus, I happen to adore you. That makes me more patient than I might be otherwise."

Kit felt a rush of affection for her agent. "Thanks, Beatrice. You're the best."

"Now go find a rich husband who can buy you a production company."

Kit groaned and tucked her phone away in her handbag. Like her mother, Beatrice was best in small doses.

Kit sat in a small classroom in Hampshire Hall for the Introduction to Psychology seminar. In addition to their lectures, the students broke into smaller groups for an hour-long seminar each week. Kit had been relieved to discover that she'd be in the same seminar group as Francie and Charlotte. She'd been disappointed, however, that the seminar would be run by Josh Hardgrave, the teaching assistant, rather than Professor Wentworth. Aside from his general unpleasant disposition, Josh seemed to have a bee in his bonnet about Kit. Probably because she'd turned him down for a date when she was sixteen. Some people could really hold a grudge.

She kept her phone inside her notebook so that she could access incoming text messages. She didn't want to miss any developments in the case. When she saw Romeo's name flash on her screen, she jumped in her seat.

"Ants in your pants, Miss Wilder?" Josh inquired with a smirk.

"Sorry, my leg fell asleep," she replied. "And at the rate we're going, the rest of me is sure to follow."

Other students giggled and Josh's face reddened. "This is a seminar where we have in-depth discussions on a given topic. Perhaps if you focus on what we're doing instead of the phone hidden in your notebook, you might be less inclined to take a nap."

Kit closed the notebook, her gaze never wavering from Josh. "Okay, Josh. Let's discuss."

The discussion consisted mainly of Josh's thoughts on common myths about psychology with a few brave voices wading into the conversation on occasion. Kit vividly remembered how much Josh liked the sound of his own voice. It was the primary reason she'd rejected his advances. Guys like Josh were a dime a dozen in Westdale and, unfortunately, the guys in Los Angeles weren't much better. That was probably why she was drawn to Romeo. He was nothing like Josh Hardgrave or Charlie Owen.

At the end of the seminar, she threw her notebook into her tote bag and rushed out the door. She was chomping at the bit to read Romeo's text.

Francie and Charlotte found her leaning against the wall, hunched over her phone.

"They think they found the owner of the muscle car," Kit told them. She'd updated them on the investigation last night on FaceTime. Francie and Charlotte seemed to be joined at the hip, which was convenient for Kit. She never had to say anything twice.

"Someone local?" Charlotte asked.

"No way," Francie replied. "I'll bet it's drugs."

Kit scanned the message. "His name is Vincent Delfino. Apparently, he's a bookie."

"Gambling," Francie corrected herself. "Close enough."

"Romeo says he frequents a couple of bars in Eastdale."

"Which ones?" Francie asked eagerly. "We should go check him out. That would be exciting."

"I'll see if I can find out," Kit promised. Anything to get this investigation over with so she could move into her new house. She missed having her own space. Despite Greyabbey's enormous size, Kit never felt like she had privacy. If it wasn't a family member or a member of staff, it was an animal nipping at her heels. Last night she got up to go to the bathroom and was followed back to her room by a duck. After the viper incident, she didn't bat an eyelid; she simply closed the door behind her and crawled back into bed.

"Have you heard of Fanatics?" Kit asked, reading Romeo's reply text. He seemed to be as glued to his phone as she was to hers.

"I think some of the guys from class hang out there on game nights," Francie commented.

"Guys from class? We should definitely go then," Charlotte said.

"You girls aren't twenty-one, though," Kit said.

"Don't need to be," Francie pointed out. "We can go in and eat and watch the game. We just can't order alcohol."

"Watch what game, exactly?" Kit asked. "Do you even know what games are on?"

Francie and Charlotte exchanged thoughtful looks. "Baseball?" Charlotte ventured slowly.

Francie nodded enthusiastically. "Yes, definitely baseball."

"Do you know anything about baseball?" Kit inquired, guessing the answer was not even remotely.

"Of course," Charlotte replied. "My father's new wife was a cheerleader for the Eagles."

Kit bit back a laugh. "Uh huh. Okay then. You can come."

Charlotte and Francie high-rived each other.

"I'll invite my cousin. He's single. We'll make a night of it."

Francie's eyebrows shot up. "Crispin?"

"Yes," Kit answered, her Cupid radar on high alert. "Crispin. I'm supposed to be spending time with family now that I'm home so two birds, one night out." Personally, she thought Crispin was a little too old for an eighteen-year-old, but her mother had been eighteen when she'd married her father. Her father had been twenty-six at the time. It did happen and, on occasion, it even lasted until death do they part. Whether his untimely death had saved them from a divorce down the road, no one could say for sure.

Kit walked through the lobby of the office building that the newspaper shared with two lawyers and an accountant. The Westdale Gazette was a small operation, but Crispin was a zealous and dedicated owner and editor. Kit had no doubt that this would have been her cousin's vocation, with or without a trust fund. Given the state of the newspaper business these days, it was probably best that Crispin had access to a trust fund.

"Kit Wilder," the receptionist said brightly.

"Hi, I'm here to see Crispin." Kit didn't recognize the young woman so assumed she was a fan of the show. That was pretty much how Kit categorized people. If they were under a certain age and she didn't know them, then they probably recognized her from television.

"I'll let him know." The receptionist picked up the phone and buzzed Crispin's office. "Your cousin is here." She hung up the phone and smiled at Kit. "One floor up, down the end of the hall on the right."

"Thanks."

"I'm a big fan," the receptionist gushed as Kit strode toward the stairs.

"Thank you," Kit called over her shoulder.

Upstairs in the hallway, she passed Myra Beacon, the realtor responsible for the sale of Ernie's house. Kit recognized her from the picture on her website. Although Beatrice and the entertainment lawyer had handled the transaction, Myra and Kit had plenty of back and forth phone calls leading up to the sale, including Kit's plea for discretion. She didn't want the world to know where she lived now.

"Kit, so nice to see you in person," Myra enthused, pumping her hand.

Kit glanced around the hall, wondering why the realtor was here. "Were you here to see Crispin?"

"Jeannie in advertising," Myra clarified. "I run weekly listings in the paper."

Kit didn't think anyone looked at real estate listings in the newspaper anymore, but what did she know?

"I heard about the dreadful business in your house," Myra said. "I'm so sorry. Obviously, I knew nothing about that."

"Of course not."

"Have you been able to live in the house at all?" Myra asked.

"No, unfortunately I'm back at Greyabbey until I get the thumbs up to move back in."

"Well, I think most people would consider themselves fortunate to live in a place like Greyabbey," Myra said wistfully. "I'd pitch a tent in the yard and feel like a million bucks there."

Kit felt the heat prick her neck. If people spent more time with Heloise Winthrop Wilder, they'd understand.

"It's Peregrine I feel sorry for," Myra said with a deep sigh. "Poor woman can't catch a break. Mind you, if I were her, I would've just gone ahead with the listing two years ago and prayed to the real estate gods for an intervention. Oh, I know I shouldn't speak ill of the dead but what a nightmare neighbor he was. His white trash version of home ownership brought down the property value of every house on the street. Anyhoo, that's all ancient history now that you're there. Who wouldn't want to live next door to Ellie Gold?"

Kit stared at the realtor, stuck on the first part of her rant. "Peregrine wanted to sell two years ago?"

"Well, yes. She's been wanting to list her house for ages so she can move to Sedona."

"But I thought that was a recent development."

"Heck no," Myra said, with a dismissive wave of her hand. "We'd finally decided to go ahead about eighteen months ago because she was desperate to leave…her sister's

101

been ill, you know. Then Ernie went and parked that motor home in the driveway." Myra shuddered at the memory. "I don't know how he could afford such a thing. Someone must've given it to him. Anyhoo, she was so thrilled when I told her that you bought it, thinking you'd spruce it up in a jiffy and she'd finally be able to sell." Myra sighed. "But then you went and found Ernie's body."

"Skeleton, technically."

Myra shrugged. "Doesn't matter to a prospective buyer. The sooner they close this investigation, the better for everyone." She leaned closer to Kit. "Speaking of which, any developments on that front?"

"I'm afraid not," Kit said, except for the one that Myra had just provided. Why would Peregrine lie to the police unless she had something to hide.

"Tell your cousin that all of us realtors appreciate him keeping it out of the papers. No need to cause unnecessary panic in Westdale. We've got to keep up appearances, after all."

Kit didn't doubt it. "See you around, Myra."

She continued to the end of the hall where Crispin's office was located. Although the door was open, she tapped on it anyway.

"Hey there," Crispin said, gesturing for her to come in. "I thought you got lost in the stairwell."

"These are nice digs," Kit said, admiring the sleek interior. The room looked more like the office of Forbes than the Westdale Gazette.

"Thanks. Feels weird that you haven't been here before."

"You weren't William Randolph Hearst the last time I was here."

Crispin grinned sheepishly. "I did like your place in L.A. I suppose you didn't keep it."

Kit shook her head. "I sold it."

"And used the proceeds to buy a murder mystery mansion."

"Hardly a mansion, but yes."

"Auntie Heloise still hasn't budged on your trust fund, huh?"

"Nope. Don't think she ever will, either. That's okay, though." Kit spun around in the swivel chair, feeling like a ten-year-old. "I'm getting my degree and building my own life."

Crispin arched an eyebrow. "Psychology, Kit? Really?"

"Did you know Josh Hardgrave is the teaching assistant for my psychology professor?"

He chuckled. "I feel sorry for the rest of the class. The two of you in one room is like a negative energy vortex."

"What's your problem with my major anyway?" Kit said in exasperation. "I expect it from my mother, but you? It's a perfectly respectable choice."

Crispin laced his fingers together. "I suppose I'm no better. My parents were mortified when I majored in journalism and bought this rag. Father thought for sure that I would work in finance."

Kit tossed a ball of rubber bands into the air and caught it. "You know what? I'm glad you didn't. I hate those guys."

Crispin nodded. "Me, too."

"So what does Frederick Breedlove do?" Not that she was interested.

Crispin laughed awkwardly. "He works for Lehman Brothers."

Kit groaned. "Great. I'll be downing gin and tonics for breakfast like my mother."

"What's the latest on the murder investigation? Everyone's very tight-lipped next door."

"Seems everyone's tight-lipped here, too," Kit remarked. "Why haven't you reported on it at all?" He opened his mouth to speak and she stopped him. "And don't give me that baloney about protecting my privacy. What's the real reason?"

Crispin squirmed under her critical gaze. "I was asked not to report on it yet."

"By whom?" Kit asked. "It's got to be Chief Riley or the mayor. They're the only people with that kind of clout." The police department was located in the town hall, which was next to Crispin's office building. The location wasn't a coincidence.

"I'm not at liberty to divulge that information," Crispin said.

Kit continued speculating. "Who am I kidding? Is it the Pilgrim Society?" She gripped the arms of the chair. "Oh God, is it Mother?"

Crispin tapped his pen on the desk. "I'll give you this much — it wasn't your mother."

"Well, it certainly wasn't Romeo...I mean, Detective Moretti."

"Romeo?" Crispin queried. "Does he look like a Romeo?"

"I don't know," Kit said. "What does a Romeo look like?"

"Like he's straight out of Verona."

"That sounds vaguely racist. Let's just say that I prefer Romeo Moretti to whatever a Breedlove is."

Crispin caught the rubber band ball as Kit tossed it in his direction. "Point taken."

"My new college friends and I are going to Eastdale tomorrow night for drinks. Care to join us?"

Crispin studied her. "Katherine Clementine Winthrop Wilder, are you trying to set me up with one of your girlfriends?"

"They're both Mayflower stock, if that sells it to you," Kit told him.

"Why Eastdale?" Crispin queried. "Why not the Weston Inn?"

"Just thought it would be nice to cross over to the dark side for a change."

"Okay then. I'm in."

"Great." Kit hesitated. "Crispin, did you know the remains are missing?"

Crispin's brow furrowed. "The skeleton took a walk?"

"Apparently. Romeo is furious. Officers Harley and Jamison were in charge of delivering the bones to the medical examiner's office. They say they left the remains, but the M.E. doesn't have it."

"Why didn't the county forensics team bring it to West Chester?"

"I don't know, Crispin. You're the journalist. Maybe you play your part in the system of checks and balances."

"Someone was paying attention in Civics class," he teased.

"I'm serious," Kit said. "Why would you ignore this story?"

He exhaled deeply. "Because Chief Riley asked me nicely," Crispin said.

"And why would he do that? Because a murder here makes him look bad?"

"The reason he gave is that he doesn't want to tip off the murderer that the investigation is underway. He says it will give them an advantage."

"Assuming the killer even reads the Westdale Gazette," Kit pointed out. "You said 'the reason he gave.' So what's the real reason?"

Crispin lowered his voice. "Off the record, I suspect it's because he's rather fond of your neighbor, Peregrine Monroe."

"Really?" Kit leaned back in her chair. "You could knock me over with a feather on that one. I can't imagine anyone being fond of Peregrine Monroe."

"Apparently, she tried to get Chief Riley to do something about the state of Ernie's house at one point."

That made sense given what she'd just heard from the realtor. "Well, he obviously didn't."

"According to my source, the chief spoke to Ernie and Ernie complained of financial trouble. He said he was behind on all his payments, including his mortgage, but that he was expecting one of his investments to pay off soon."

"My neighbors seem to think he ran through money like it was water. Did Chief Riley believe him?"

Crispin shrugged. "I think he felt sorry for him. It's hard to watch someone's life unravel."

"I don't know if it unraveled as much as Ernie pulled his own threads." Sadly, Kit realized that she could relate to the dead man. It wasn't a pleasant thought.

Chapter Seven

Fanatics was a sports bar on the outskirts of Eastdale. The Phillies were playing on three of the wide-screened televisions and the noise level in the bar rose and fell with each swing of the bat.

Kit wound her way through the crowd, praying that no one recognized her. Based on the audience demographics, she had a feeling that there were plenty of Fool's Gold fans in this group. The fact that she wore her brown hair loose down her back was helpful. Ellie's hair was usually slicked back in a no-nonsense ponytail.

"I withdraw my vote for a night on the dark side. Why in God's name would you choose this place?" Crispin hissed. "Crossing the bridge into Eastdale is bad enough. I saw a guy wearing socks with sandals."

"You like sports," she replied.

"I like cricket and tennis," he snapped. "Not pot-bellied old men squatting behind a plate. They look like they're fed a diet of Twinkies and hot dogs."

"When you put it that way, it does seem unappealing," Kit agreed. She had no particular feelings on the subject of baseball. Her mother didn't follow any sports teams and her father had watched Wimbledon, the US Open and the Kentucky Derby. That was about it.

The rooms were so loud and crowded that Kit wondered if she'd be able to talk to Vincent Delfino even if he was there.

"Someone's waving to you," Crispin said, tapping her on the shoulder and gesturing to a table in the back room. "Judging by the Hermes bag on the table, I'm guessing they're your friends."

"You're the only straight guy I know who would recognize an Hermes bag," Kit said.

"Huntley would."

"The jury's still out on Huntley," Kit replied as she squeezed her way to the table.

"Kit, you made it," Francie said, standing to air kiss each cheek.

"This is my cousin, Crispin Winthrop," Kit said.

"You both look familiar," Crispin told them, now that he was up close.

"I've seen you around," Francie said, "but we've never been formally introduced. I'm Francie Musgrove and this is Charlotte Tilton."

"Ah," Crispin said, "I should certainly recognize a Musgrove when I see one." Crispin pointed at Charlotte. "And I know your sister, Rebecca. And your father, of course. How is he?"

Charlotte studied the napkin in her lap. "He's not great, but we're all praying for him."

Crispin took the seat next to Charlotte. "I'm sorry to hear that. He's a good man."

"Crispin runs the Westdale Gazette," Kit mentioned in an effort to change the subject.

"Can I get you all some drinks from the bar?" the waitress asked. She was dressed in a tight half-shirt and denim shorts. Kit thought about some of the skimpy outfits she'd worn on television and quickly recognized that she and the Fanatics waitress weren't very different from each other. It was just that Kit had been paid a lot more money.

"I'd like an old fashioned," Crispin said.

The waitress studied him. "Funny, you don't look eighty years old."

"How about a French 75?" Francie suggested. "My family practically lives on it."

"I don't even know what that is," the waitress snapped. "How about you try a beer? Hot day like this one, I bet you'll find it refreshing."

Crispin loosened his collar. "I'll have a martini, neat."

The waitress looked him up and down. "Shocker." She turned to Kit. "And you?"

"I'll try a local ale," she said, ignoring Crispin's critical look.

"We'll have iced tea, no lemons, and a basket of cheese fries," Francie said.

The waitress flashed her teeth at Francie. "You won't regret the cheese fries…at least not while you're eating them." With those parting words, she retreated to the back of the bar.

Kit took a moment to survey the room. She had no clue what Vincent Delfino looked like. Her Google search had turned up a priest in New York and a college student at the University of Miami with an interesting Snapchat profile. Any one of these beer-swilling, denim-wearing guys could be Vincent Delfino, the bookie.

"See anyone worth talking to?" Charlotte asked, noticing Kit's wandering gaze.

Francie gripped her arm. "Ooh, do you see the criminal?"

"What criminal?" Crispin asked. He cast a suspicious glance in Kit's direction. "What are we really doing here?"

"We're breaking free of our Westdale chains, obviously," Francie said quickly. "Someone in our class mentioned that this was a good place to hang out."

"Are you sure you weren't talking to the janitor?" Crispin asked, wrinkling his nose.

Kit laughed. "I have missed you, Crispin. Listen, I need the restroom. Can you entertain my friends while I'm gone?"

Francie offered an appealing smile and Crispin softened. "Of course."

On her way to the restroom, Kit spied the waitress coming out of a back room.

"Excuse me," Kit said, getting her attention with a wave. "I'm looking for Vincent Delfino. Any chance he's here tonight?"

The waitress sucked in her cheeks. "I say this out of the kindness of my heart. Go back to Westdale and stick to the country club circuit."

"I'm not here to make a bet," Kit said. "I'm looking for someone and I think he might know where he is." Like under the floorboards in her house.

The waitress jerked her head toward the nearest bar. Kit spotted a dark-haired man in a white Phillies T-shirt and jeans standing between two other men on bar stools. They were all riveted to the television. The Phillies scored and the crowd erupted. Delfino punched his own hand in a triumphant gesture.

Kit made her move while he still appeared euphoric. She didn't want to take so long that her friends came in search of her and ruined the moment.

She maneuvered her way between Delfino and the man to his right and smiled at the busy bartender who wasn't even looking in her direction. She felt Delfino's gaze on her but kept her eyes on the bartender.

"Troy always hangs out down there," Delfino said, nodding toward the other end of the bar. "I think you can see why."

Kit noticed a group of attractive young women huddled en masse. A collection of beer bottles sat on the bar top and Troy was deep in conversation with the redhead.

"I prefer brunettes, myself," Delfino said, trying to catch her eye.

Kit decided it was time to play and faced him. "Is that so?" Although his eyes were dark like Romeo's, they lacked the sparkle. And the eyelashes. Romeo's eyelashes deserved their own Twitter account. Kit pinched her own leg to keep herself focused. Now was not the time to ponder Romeo's dreamy eyes.

"Wow, anybody ever tell you you're gorgeous?" Delfino cooed.

Oh, only about five hundred thousand people. "Thank you," she said and lowered her eyes demurely. He was more likely to talk if he thought she was the quiet type. At least, that's what the writers of Fool's Gold believed.

"You new here? I definitely haven't seen you before." The way he drank her in made Kit feel desperate for a shower. He obviously wasn't a fan of the show. There was no sign of recognition in his expression. She had to admit, she was mildly surprised. He seemed to fit the demographic.

"I just moved into a house in Westdale," she replied. She hated to give her real address, but she thought it was the best way to crack him.

"No shit," he said. "I know Westdale like the back of my hand. Where at?"

"Thornhill Road," she answered and watched his reaction carefully.

"I know that street," he said brightly. "A friend of mine lived there."

Lived. Past tense.

"Which house?" she asked.

"I don't remember the house number. Ernie Ludwig's his name."

"I'm afraid I don't know him," she said. "Did he move?"

"Something like that," Delfino said vaguely and took a swig of his beer.

Despite Delfino's evasiveness, Kit wasn't getting a murderous vibe from him. To be honest, she wasn't even getting a lecherous vibe from him. She'd expected a creep, but he seemed okay for a knee-busting bookie. She didn't want to date him, but she got the sense that he didn't belong behind bars either.

"What are you drinking?" Delfino asked.

Kit glanced at the cluster of bottles down the far end of the bar. "Dogfish Head," she said.

"Excellent taste." He cupped his hands around his mouth. "Yo Troy, stop making babies down there and get this lady a drink."

Troy reluctantly tore himself away from the redhead. When he caught sight of Kit, his eyes widened in recognition. She quickly brought a finger to her lips and shook her head. If Delfino didn't recognize her, she didn't want him to know her name.

"Hi," he stammered, staring at Kit. "Wow, what can I get you?"

"My lady friend would like a Dogfish ale, please," Delfino ordered for her.

"On the house, Miss," Troy said with a wink.

Delfino smiled and gave Kit a sidelong glance. "See? He thinks you're gorgeous, too."

Kit started to feel guilty for stringing Delfino along. He probably thought he had a sure thing going on.

Troy popped the lid and poured the beer in a pint glass for Kit.

"Classy," Delfino commented. "Let me pay for it, Troy."

The bartender waved him off. "Nah, I told you. On the house."

Delfino shrugged. "Next one's on me."

"Great," a deep voice interjected. "I got here just in time then."

Kit craned her neck and nearly spat out her beer in Delfino's face when she saw Romeo standing behind her.

"Enjoying yourself?" he asked Kit. Despite the friendly question, he did not look happy to see her.

"I made a new friend," Kit said weakly.

Delfino glanced from Kit to the very tall, very buff Romeo. "You two know each other?" he asked, clearly hoping the answer was no.

"We only met recently," Kit said since that was the truth. She turned to Romeo. "Mr. Delfino was just telling me how familiar he is with my street."

Delfino's eyes narrowed. "How'd you know my name?" He looked quickly from Kit to Romeo.

Romeo sighed loudly as Kit winced. Rookie mistake. In fact, Ellie had done the same thing in episode two of season one. She'd ended up tied to a chair in a warehouse in that episode, but she doubted that would be the outcome now. Not with Romeo behind her.

"Is there somewhere quiet we can talk?" Romeo asked politely.

Kit half expected Delfino to make a run for it, but to his credit, he nodded and headed toward a side door.

"You stay here," Romeo ordered her when she started to follow them.

"No, I'm coming," Kit insisted. "I want to hear what he says." She paused. "He's nice so don't hurt him."

Romeo shook his head in frustration. "Come on, Nancy Drew."

The three of them ended up in an alley on the side of the building. At least it was well-lit, Kit decided as she scoped the area. Her phone began to play Semi-Charmed Life by Third Eye Blind and she knew it was Crispin trying to figure out what on earth happened to her.

"Hi," she said. "I'll be back in a minute."

"Where are you?" Crispin demanded. "The drinks have been here for ages."

"I said I'll be back," she huffed and hung up.

Romeo shot her a quizzical look.

"I didn't come alone," she explained.

That response didn't seem to please him either. Kit was zero for two. If she'd learned anything from her brief exposure to baseball, it was that one more strike meant she was out.

"So I get that you're a cop," Delfino said, nodding at Romeo. "But who are you?"

"She just plays one on TV," Romeo said.

Delfino took it as a joke. "Well, she's pretty enough. That's for sure."

"So you've never seen Fool's Gold?" Kit asked. She couldn't resist the question. As much as she tried to fight her ego, it had a habit of overpowering her at inopportune moments. Like this one.

Delfino scratched his chin. "The movie with that guy who's always running around shirtless? Matthew something?"

Kit gritted her teeth. "No, not a movie. The television show."

"I only watch sports." He grinned. "For obvious reasons."

"Okay," Romeo said impatiently. "I'm here to ask you about Ernie Ludwig. I understand he placed bets with you."

Delfino didn't even try to deny his bookie role. "Why do I get the idea you got bigger fish to fry?"

"Right now I'm trying to figure out if you're the bigger fish," Romeo said.

Delfino blinked in confusion. "What's going on? Ernie skipped town last year and I haven't seen him since."

"That must've pissed you off since he owed you a lot of money," Romeo said.

"It didn't exactly make me happy," Delfino admitted. "He owed me for the SuperBowl and March Madness."

Romeo whistled. "That is a lot of dough. Did you stop by before he left town? Maybe personally deliver him a message?"

Delfino shook his head adamantly. "I'm not into that, ask anybody. I'm a businessman and sometimes I take a loss." He shrugged. "That's the cost of doing business."

Romeo didn't appear convinced. "Are you telling me that you didn't go to Ernie's house before he disappeared?"

"No," Delfino insisted. "I don't do house calls."

"I have a witness that ID'd your car on Thornhill Road the week Ernie disappeared."

"Lots of people drive a car like mine." He straightened. "It's very trendy."

"Vincent," Kit said softly, "you told me that you know my street well. That Ernie was your friend."

"I didn't say I've never been there," Delfino argued. "I'm saying I didn't go there to rough him up and I didn't go there the week he disappeared."

"How do you know you weren't there the week he disappeared?" Romeo queried. "That implies that you know exactly when he disappeared."

Delfino appeared thoughtful. "I know when he left town because we were supposed to meet up. He said he was going to pay me, but he never showed."

"So you drove by his house to check on him," Romeo prompted.

Delfino's shoulders sagged. "Yeah, okay, I drove by. When I saw the motor home was gone, I knew he'd taken off. I didn't even bother to get out of the car."

Kit bit her lip. Why was the motor home gone? Did the murderer drive off in it so that he had somewhere to hide out? Somewhere that could hit the road whenever necessary? Or was it evidence? She'd need to ask Romeo about that later.

"Do I need a lawyer?" Delfino asked, shoving his hands into his pockets.

"Not right now," Romeo advised. Delfino looked relieved.

"Shouldn't you tell him not to leave town in case you have more questions?" Kit inquired.

"That's what phones are for," Romeo said.

"Speaking of phones," Delfino said with a hopeful look at Kit, "can I get your digits?"

"Sorry," Romeo said, placing a proprietary hand on Kit's arm. "It's against the rules." He took Kit by the arm and walked her down the alley to the front of the building.

"What rules?" Kit asked.

"Were you seriously considering giving that guy your number?" Romeo asked.

"Well, he already knows my address," Kit said.

"What?" Romeo exploded. He gripped Kit's arm. "Kit, what do you think you're doing? This isn't a Hollywood set. The director isn't going to yell cut if you get yourself into a situation that you can't handle."

"I've never been in a situation that I can't handle," she told him boldly.

He took her phone from her pocket and held it out to her. "Call the guy you're here with and tell him you're leaving."

Kit brushed her fingers over his as she retrieved her phone. She felt the crackle of electricity between them and she could tell by the expression on his face that he felt it, too.

"I'll text him," she said.

She texted Crispin to meet her out front with the girls. She figured he wouldn't be too upset about leaving the noisy sports bar sooner than expected.

"I'll wait with you until he comes out," Romeo said gruffly.

Checking out the competition, Kit thought to herself with amusement.

"So do you think Delfino did it?" she asked.

"No," he replied. "But since I don't know who did, he stays on the list." He looked squarely at Kit and his expression softened. "Why did you come here to interrogate him? Do you not trust me to do my job?"

His face was so aggrieved that Kit felt a flash of guilt. Of course she thought he was capable. More than capable.

"Well, you know how much I want to move back in," she said, "but I also feel a sense of responsibility. I'm the one who found Ernie. It seems only right that I should help find his killer. I don't like the idea of Ernie haunting me at night. He doesn't sound like the ideal ghost."

Romeo suppressed a smile. "How about this? You stop interviewing suspects and I'll let you back in your house."

Kit lit up. "Really?"

119

"Here you are," Crispin said. He sounded relieved and Kit guessed it was because he was able to leave Fanatics without looking like a snob.

"We were getting worried," Francie added.

"Is that why you ate most of the cheese fries?" Charlotte asked.

Francie shrugged. "I'm a stress eater."

Romeo eyed Kit. "You were with these three?"

"Romeo, meet my cousin, Crispin Winthrop. And these are my friends from school, Francie and Charlotte." She faced her friends. "This is Detective Moretti. He's leading the investigation into Ernie's murder."

Romeo broke into a wide grin as he gave Crispin's hand an enthusiastic shake. "Good to meet you."

"Crispin owns the Westdale Gazette," Kit said. She felt like Crispin should wear a sign so that she could stop telling people.

Francie and Charlotte were staring dreamily at Romeo so Kit snapped her fingers at them. "Back to earth, ladies."

"So is Kit as big of a pain in class as she is in real life?" Romeo asked.

Kit elbowed him in the ribs. "You don't want to get on my bad side," she warned.

Crispin grew serious. "You really don't. She has a roundhouse kick that will send you back five years."

"Spoken like someone who knows," Romeo said.

"Not me, but there's a certain ex-boyfriend with the scar to prove it." Crispin didn't say Charlie Owen's name, but Kit knew that was the ex-boyfriend at issue. He'd deserved it, too.

"Can we talk tomorrow?" Kit asked Romeo. "I have other information that might be useful."

Romeo arched a thick eyebrow. "Please don't tell me there have been others."

"Not like Delfino," she promised.

"Where would you like to meet? The coffee shop?"

"How about my house since you're letting me back in it?"

Romeo gave her hand a squeeze and immediately released it. "Sure. Your house at ten. I'll bring the donuts and coffee."

Kit rolled her eyes. "Nothing like a good stereotype."

The front door was open when Romeo arrived at the house on Thornhill Road. Kit didn't hear the deep timbre of his voice. She was too engrossed in unpacking a box of pots and pans in the kitchen and dancing wildly to Taylor Swift's Blank Space.

As Taylor sang about how young and reckless she was, Kit spun around with a cast iron pan in her hand and nearly whacked Romeo in the chest. Judging from the way he looked in a fitted black T-shirt, Kit was pretty sure the pan would've shattered into pieces if it had made contact.

Quickly, she pulled out her ear buds. "Sorry, I didn't hear you come in."

She noticed his scowl. "Do you really think it's wise to leave your door wide open now that you've given your address to a known criminal?"

She ignored his rebuke. "I believe I was promised donuts and coffee."

Romeo inclined his head. "On the mantle."

Kit made a beeline for the living room. "I hope you didn't get jelly. I hate the jelly kind." She opened the box and peered inside. "Why do we have so many unhealthy yet delicious options on this coast?" She plucked a cinnamon donut from the box.

Romeo brought the two coffees into the kitchen and Kit followed.

"Delfino's harmless," she said, picking up the thread of their conversation.

"I told you last night that he's still on the list. Not all murders are intentional. He could've killed Ludwig by accident and then panicked."

"I'll believe it when you show me the evidence."

"So you're a judge now?" Romeo surveyed the pile of open boxes on the kitchen floor. "Boy, you didn't waste any time."

"I told you I wanted to come home." She put her hands on her hips and scrutinized the boxes. "I would offer you a plate, but I don't know where they are."

In one swift move, Romeo plucked two plates from a nearby box and handed them to her.

"Impressive. What's your next trick?" she quipped as she arranged the donuts on the plates.

Romeo shifted a few boxes so that he could sit down at the small table by the sliding glass door. "Before we continue this conversation, I want you to promise me that you'll stay away from Vincent Delfino."

Kit opened the lid of her coffee and sipped. "I'm not planning to date him, if that's what you're worried about."

He waved her off. "I mean it, Kit. Stay out of police business. Whatever you did on your show isn't the same as real life. People aren't following a script."

"I know. If they were, Delfino would've groped me or been a much bigger creep than he actually was."

Romeo sighed. "You're not making this easy."

She chomped on her donut. "You'll change your mind about that when you hear what I know."

Romeo leaned back in his chair. "I'm almost afraid to ask."

"Did you know that Peregrine Monroe wanted to sell her house, like, two years ago?"

"And?"

"Why didn't she tell us that? As far as anyone knows, that's a recent development. And why do you think she didn't list her house?"

Romeo nodded, understanding. "Her mess of a neighbor."

"Exactly. She even tried to get Chief Riley to speak to him."

"Chief Riley?" The wheels began turning. "Let me guess. They're both Pilgrims."

Kit snorted. "Chief Riley? Not quite. He's sweet on her."

Romeo stretched his legs and stood. "Can I help you unpack? I'm uncomfortable sitting here with all these boxes."

Kit was taken aback. A guy who was proactive and wanted to pitch in? Was he a new species? "Sure. Why don't you remove the risk of me hitting you with pots and pans by putting those in the lower cabinets?" She pointed to the largest box on the floor.

Romeo set to work. "So is Peregrine the reason why the press hasn't reported the murder?"

"You noticed the lack of press coverage, huh?"

"Your cousin," Romeo said, sliding a steamer to the back of the shelf. "You said he runs the paper, right?"

Kit nodded and pulled a Vitamix from the box. "Thank God." She hugged the blender to her chest.

Romeo glanced at her discovery. "Your version of a teddy bear?" he queried.

"I miss the kale smoothies I make with this baby."

Romeo scrunched his nose. "You really were in Hollywood, weren't you?"

Kit unearthed an omelette pan from the bottom of the box. "Hey, have you made any progress on the murder weapon? What do you think crushed his chest?"

"We've been searching the storage unit with Ernie's belongings but haven't found anything yet."

"Who pays for the unit?" Kit wondered.

"The bank. Once we're finished our investigation, though, they'll sell the stuff. You've seen those shows on TV, right? Where people bid on the contents of a unit."

Kit shook her head. "No. Sounds boring."

Romeo chuckled. "I agree, but my dad loves those shows." He flattened his empty box and moved on to another one.

"Why is the bank still holding his stuff after all this time?"

"Red tape," Romeo replied. "You can always count on red tape when there's a bank involved. They're worse than the government."

"But just as crooked," Kit remarked. "So why do you think the killer took the motor home?"

"We can't say with certainty that he did."

"But what's the other option?" Kit pressed him. "Someone happened to steal it around the same time Ernie was killed?"

"I agree it's unlikely." Romeo held up a mug in the shape of a pig. "One of yours?"

Kit swiped the mug from his hands and clutched it protectively. "I collect pigs. So what?" Carefully, she placed the mug on the windowsill behind the sink.

"We haven't found any sign of the motor home, but it'll be tough to locate, especially if the tags have been switched."

"Why didn't anyone look for Ernie when he went missing last year?" she asked. She felt a sudden rush of sympathy for the unpopular neighbor. At least if she went missing, people would notice. Heck, people noticed if she went four hours without tweeting.

"No one ever reported him missing," Romeo said. "His house was already on the verge of foreclosure when he supposedly left town. He owed a lot of money to Delfino. Seems to me everyone assumed he took off in his motor home and started a new life somewhere else."

Kit stared at the Tiffany bud vase in her hand. It had been a Valentine's Day gift from the two-timing Charlie Owen. "But he was here the whole time." She pushed the vase to the back of the shelf.

"Why are you storing that?" Romeo reached in and rescued the vase from the back of the cabinet. "It's beautiful." His dark eyes twinkled. "I'll be right back."

Two minutes later, he reappeared with a single pink rose. He filled the vase with water and popped the rose inside.

"Voila," he said, placing the vase in the middle of her small table.

Kit was touched. "You didn't steal that from Thora's prizewinning garden, did you?"

"Technically, it was on your property," he said with a sheepish grin.

"Be careful. She probably has surveillance cameras pointed at her rose garden."

"I wish she did. Then we could watch old videos for clues." He returned to the box of mugs. "I think your cousin should report on the discovery of the body."

"Why? Chief Riley doesn't want residents to panic."

"No, it seems Chief Riley wants to protect the property values of certain members of the community. It's not in the public interest to keep this quiet."

Kit studied him. "You think it might flush out the killer?"

Romeo shrugged. "I'd be curious to see how our suspects respond to the news when it goes public. He's got an online version, too, right?"

"What do you think people actually read?" she said archly.

"I'll stop by his office when I leave here. I'd like it to run as soon as possible."

"Have the bones turned up?" she asked.

126

He scowled again. "I'm beginning to think Chief Riley had a hand in that, too."

"And a foot and even a torso," Kit added grimly. If Romeo was right, then the Westdale Police brought a whole new meaning to the phrase 'to serve and protect.'

Kit rode Peppermint along the rough grounds of Greyabbey. The sun was high and hot and she was regretting her decision to take the horse out on such a sweltering day.

"Hey, Miss Wilder," a voice called and Kit noticed Paul Krasensky ambling toward her.

"Hi, Paul," she said. She steered Peppermint alongside him.

"This is good timing," Paul said. "I'll be able to check her over as soon as you bring her back."

"How's everything in the Krasensky family?" she asked.

"You know, same crap, different day. The twins ain't speaking because of a boy." He rolled his eyes. "So I got Janine in my spare room and now I got my younger brother crashing on my sofa. Never a dull moment."

"Well, it looks like my neighbor is selling her house soon if any Krasenskys are interested. It's the cleanest house you've ever seen. It's on the corner of Thornhill and Keystone Roads." She doubted the price would be right for them, but she wouldn't mind having a Krasensky for a neighbor. They seemed like the sort of loud, argumentative family that she's always longed to be a part of.

Paul scratched his chin. "Peregrine Monroe's finally selling her place, huh?"

"What do you mean 'finally'?" Kit couldn't imagine how Paul would be privy to such information.

"She was hoping to sell ages ago. She'd paid Carl a tidy sum to…" He stopped talking and spat on the ground. "Forget it."

"Paul, tell me," she urged. Although Peppermint was growing antsy standing still, she wasn't ready to finish the conversation. "What did she pay Carl to do?"

He stared at the ground. "I don't know exactly, but whatever it was, she paid enough for Carl to start over somewhere new. That's what he always wanted. He hated the winter. Always talked about going somewhere like Arizona."

The gears in Kit's mind began to shift. "Did he have a car?"

Paul shook his head. "Nope, he had a bike, but mostly he walked unless he needed to go into Philly or something. Then he'd take the train."

Kit tried to keep her breathing steady. "Paul, I know you said you and Carl don't keep in regular contact, but when was the last time you heard from him?"

"Not sure. I think it was right after Tommy's birthday last year. We went to Fanatics and watched the Phillies." Paul gazed up at her, shielding his eyes from the bright sun. "You think maybe he hurt the guy and took off?"

Killed him and took off in his motor home, you mean, Kit thought to herself. It made sense that he wouldn't make contact with his family. Carl was probably laying low until the dust settled. She didn't have the heart to call Carl a murderer to his brother's innocent face, though. Maybe she didn't want a Krasensky living next door after all.

"I honestly don't know, Paul. I'll give Detective Moretti a call and let him know it's time for another conversation with Peregrine Monroe."

"I don't want to get Carl in any trouble," Paul said. Kit could see the worry lines deepening in his forehead.

"If he didn't do anything wrong, he won't get in trouble."

"Oh, I'm sure he did something wrong," Paul admitted. "He's my brother and I love him, but being a thug kept him from being penniless. I don't think he would kill anybody, though. Not on purpose anyway."

"Would you be willing to talk to the police? Tell them everything you know?" she asked, fully aware that she was putting him in a difficult position. If Peregrine Monroe denied hiring Carl, the police would need Paul's statement to contradict her.

Paul looked away from Kit in the direction of Greyabbey. "Family's everything, you know? Even if we don't like the people we're tied to, we're still bonded for life."

Kit realized that Paul wasn't going to help willingly. She dismounted and offered him the reins. "Would you mind taking her back? I'm not in the mood to ride anymore."

Wordlessly, Paul took the reins and slunk toward the stable. As much as she liked Paul, she couldn't withhold the information from the police. Not when it seemed like the information could lead to the murderer.

On the walk back to Greyabbey, Kit decided to call Romeo. She didn't want to delay passing along Paul's pertinent information.

"You just can't enough of me," he answered. "Not that I blame you."

"I know I'm not supposed to be involving myself, especially now that I get to live in my house," she began, "but I have a tip for you."

"Let me guess. Delfino came by with a picnic lunch and a signed confession."

"Jealous?" she teased. He certainly sounded jealous.

"Please tell me it doesn't involve the bookie." She could practically hear him frowning.

"It doesn't." She told him about Carl Krasenky's possible involvement.

Romeo blew out a loud, exasperated breath. "I guess it's time to pay Peregrine Monroe another visit." He paused. "Alone, this time."

"You want me to talk to her by myself?" Kit asked.

"Ha ha. Not funny. I'll speak to her without you, thanks."

"That's my reward for helping out? A time-out in the penalty box?"

"It can't be a time-out when you don't belong in the game in the first place," Romeo explained.

"Fine, have it your way." She saw Hermes and Valentino bounding toward her. "I should go. Someone's released the hounds."

"Tell your cousin thanks for the coverage, by the way. I read the article this morning."

"In print or online?" she queried, fending off Valentino's sloppy kisses.

"In the paper over an espresso in Butter Beans."

Kit's radar pinged. "You were in Butter Beans? Why would you come to Westdale for your morning coffee?" For a moment, she thought it might be for the chance to run into her. She quickly realized her mistake. "You were eavesdropping."

"Maybe."

"Hear anything good?"

"Not that I'd share with a civilian who is most definitely not a part of this case. And just a warning, you may get some looky-loos on your front lawn now that the word is out."

"I'm used to unwanted eyeballs," she replied. Not that she liked it.

"So Carl's brother is Paul?" he asked. "I'd like to speak to him sooner rather than later."

"He's at the stable now, but I suspect he won't be by the time you get here. He doesn't seem eager to rat out his brother."

"Do you have an address for him?"

"No, but I can get it from Huntley."

"No, I'll get it from him. You're not involved, remember?"

She remembered well enough, but somebody needed to clue in the universe because it clearly wasn't listening.

Chapter Eight

Kit pulled her hair back into a ponytail and slipped on a hat as she prepared to cut the grass in her backyard. She wasn't entirely sure how to operate the mower, but Thora had assured her that it was easy like Sunday morning. Thora was apparently a Lionel Richie fan. The older woman had a lawn service that came once a week so she'd offered Kit the use of her old mower. Kit had never done anything so domestic in her life. At Greyabbey and in Los Angeles, she'd had staff for such tasks. As a college student with her own fixer upper, however, it was time to learn the basics.

She started the mower and began guiding it in a straight line across the lawn. No pushing was required. The mower practically moved by itself. It didn't take long before Kit grew bored of cutting neat rows. She made a tight turn and cut diagonally across the yard. Then she carried on criss-crossing her way around the lawn, starting to enjoy herself.

The faint ringing of a bell tickled her ear and she stopped the mower to listen.

"That's the craziest technique I've ever seen," Thora remarked from her side of the yard. In her hand, she held a delicate silver bell.

"Not so much a technique as a pattern."

"Can I offer you a lemonade?" Thora asked. "You look like you need hydration, not to mention another twenty pounds."

"Lemonade sounds perfect."

Kit surveyed the neatly cut star shape as she walked across the lawn and was pleased with her handiwork. She thought it was interesting that, as much as Peregrine and Thora disliked Ernie, neither had erected a fence between their properties. Maybe this was a situation where good fences would have made good neighbors, although Kit doubted it.

"That's a beautiful bell," Kit said.

Thora handed it over for closer inspection. "A Mayflower heirloom."

Why would the Pilgrims have brought bells? She knew they'd brought necessities like hatchets and pots and pans but bells? Kit doubted its authenticity.

"Do you use it often?" As old as Thora was, Kit couldn't imagine how an antique bell featured into the woman's everyday life.

"Mainly to annoy family members," she replied, her eyes twinkling. "You should see my niece's face when I hand this baby over to her son." She chuckled to herself. "Headaches all around."

"You should try a bullhorn," Kit suggested.

Thora gave her a scornful look. "Not terribly genteel, is it?"

Yes, it's more polite to annoy your family with a dainty antique, Kit thought with amusement.

She followed Thora through the back door and into the kitchen where two glasses of lemonade awaited them.

"So what's the latest with the investigation?" Thora asked, settling into a chair at the table.

"Nothing concrete," Kit replied. "The most recent lead was a bust."

"Oh." Her mouth drooped. "I thought maybe you'd cracked it since you were allowed to move back in."

Kit took a big swallow of lemonade and immediately regretted it. There must have been a cup of sugar in there. It took all of her acting ability to hide her disgust.

"No," she answered with a slight croak. "The police were finished at the house so they said I could come back."

Thora swirled her lemonade around in her glass. "Have they found the motor home?"

Kit shook her head. "Not that I know of. They're looking, of course, but they figure the license plate was removed or replaced right after the murder." Kit wondered why Thora was pumping her for information. "You could speak to the police directly, you know. I'm sure Chief Riley would be happy to put your mind at ease. He seems to love talking to the ladies of Westdale."

Thora waved her off. "Poppycock. He's not the eyes and ears of this investigation." She took a sip of lemonade and smacked her lips. "You are."

The older woman wasn't wrong. Chief Riley was too busy schmoozing residents over at the country club to adequately handle a murder investigation. His expertise was limited to parking tickets and neighborly disputes. That was the reason Romeo was involved in the first place. According to Romeo, the Westdale police were more than happy to leave the heavy lifting to Romeo and his team.

"Would you like a slice of pie?" Thora asked. "I picked up fresh cherries from the farmer's market this weekend." The weekly market was held on Westdale Green, the open space adjacent to the college grounds.

"I won't say no to pie," Kit said. As Thora hobbled to her feet, Kit stopped her. "I'll get it. Just tell me where it is."

Thora sank back into her chair. "My arthritis is acting up again. I think it's the humidity."

Kit spotted the pie on the counter next to the refrigerator. "Looks delicious."

"I'm guessing you don't eat much pie from the look of you."

Kit took two plates from a cabinet and opened the drawer for a knife and forks. "I'll admit, I'm a healthy eater, but I also exercise a lot so I can afford the occasional…" She was about to say 'splurge' but the item in the drawer caught her off guard.

"Wrong drawer, dear," Thora said. "The cutlery is in the drawer to your left."

Kit continued to stare in the drawer. Finally, she gripped the item and held it up for Thora to see. "Does this work?"

Thora squinted. "Of course it does. It's a Derringer."

Dear Lord, Thora owned firearms? The thought made Kit uncomfortable. She placed the handgun back in the drawer. "How old is it?"

Thora tapped the table thoughtfully. "I honestly can't remember. It was a gift from my first husband."

"Was your first husband a sheriff in the Wild West?"

Thora smiled dreamily. "It has a beautiful gold inlaid barrel band. It's very rare."

"Have you ever fired it?" Kit couldn't tear her eyes from the Derringer. It looked more like a movie prop than a real, working gun.

"Why would I have a gun if I didn't intend to shoot it?"

Kit raised her eyebrows but said nothing. She located the cutlery drawer and pulled out two forks and a knife.

"Don't tell me you're one of those bleeding heart liberals that wants me to be murdered in my sleep?" Thora clucked her tongue. "That's what Hollywood does to a perfectly good conservative girl."

"Well, if you're really worried about being murdered in your sleep, why is your weapon of choice in the kitchen drawer next to the birthday candles? Shouldn't it be closer to your bed?"

Kit brought two slices of cherry pie over to the table. Thora frowned as Kit set a plate in front of her.

"That's not a generous piece," she complained.

"And you accused me of not being conservative," Kit replied, popping a forkful of pie into her mouth. It was a perfect blend of sweet and tart, not unlike its creator.

The sound of shattered glass jolted Kit awake. She leaped from her bed in a state of confusion. She wasn't sure if the sound came from her house or next door. She kept the light off and crept to the open window to peer outside. Her own backyard appeared dark and quiet.

Kit snaked her way down the hall and then the staircase, careful not step on any creaky floorboards. The eerie silence unnerved her. If someone was in her house, they were in stealth mode.

She kept her back to the wall and made her way to the kitchen at the back of the house. There was no sign of an intruder. Once in the kitchen, she lifted her cell phone from the kitchen table and turned it. Her heart was pounding but she knew she had to check next door. She was certain that the sound of breaking glass was not part of some dream.

Kit unlocked the back door and stepped into the darkness. She decided to check Thora's house first. May as well start with the neighbor she liked. She hurried across the stretch of lawn that joined the two properties, staying close to the back of Thora's house. She saw shards of glass dangling in the window frame and her heart contracted. She darted back across the lawn and into her own house, locking the door behind her.

Breathing heavily, she began to text Romeo out of habit but quickly realized that the Westdale Police would be closer, if less competent.

"9-1-1, what is your emergency?" a nasal voice asked.

"Someone has broken into my neighbor's house. Please hurry. She's an old...I mean, mature woman and lives alone." For a fleeting moment, Kit wondered if she would one day share Thora's fate. The old lady with a reputation for crazy who lived alone with her antique guns and cherry pies. Poor Thora didn't even own a cat to eat her face when she died. Life was so unfair.

Kit gave the dispatcher the address and hung up. Next she texted Romeo, in case emergency services took too long. She doubted he was awake, let alone dressed for a quick drive to Westdale, but she was willing to risk annoying her favorite detective if it meant saving Thora from harm.

After a minute of pacing and complete silence outside, she called Jordan. Not only was he on California time, but Jordan was also an insomniac, a fact that came in handy on occasion.

"What's new, pussycat? Wait, don't tell me," Jordan said. "You've found another body."

"I might in five minutes if the police don't hurry up and get here."

"What happened?" he asked, sensing her urgency.

"Someone just broke into my neighbor's house through a back window," she told him. "I called the police but Westdale's finest are slower than a one-legged tortoise."

"So grab a weapon and get over there," Jordan urged her. "Your old lady neighbor might be helpless, but you're not."

Only Jordan would encourage Kit to risk her life at the drop of a hat. He'd always believed in her, to his credit and her detriment.

"I don't have any weapons," she replied. "I'm not an actual cop, remember?"

"Okay, what about episode four, season three," he said, trying to jog her memory. "The one that guest starred the guy from CSI."

Kit's eyes sparkled. "Yes, the one with the jewel heist."

"That's the one. Ellie happens to be inside that upscale jewelry store that's a cross between Van Cleef & Arpels and…"

"Jordan, I am about to confront a criminal," Kit hissed. "Get to the point."

"Well, the robbers have taken the owner hostage and Ellie has to take them on by herself."

"She shoots a chandelier that falls on the guy's head!" Kit took a deep breath in an effort to calm her nerves and slid her feet into her white bunny slippers. "Wait, what does that have to do with my situation?"

"Does your neighbor have a chandelier?"

Kit smacked her forehead. "I can't wait anymore. Cover me, I'm going in."

"Keep me on speaker phone," Jordan suggested. "That way I can call the police if something happens."

"I've already called the police," Kit reminded him.

"Good point. Then just keep me on speaker phone so I can listen."

Kit groaned. He was the worst voyeur she knew. Even so, she kept him on the line for her own sanity, tucking the phone into the waistband of her heart-covered pajama shorts.

She grabbed a throw from her sofa before heading back to Thora's. She placed the blanket over the broken glass before climbing into the house. There'd be no saving Thora if Kit sliced her femoral artery.

"Kit, what's going on? I can't see. Wait, are those the heart pjs that Charlie bought for you?" Jordan's whisper was muffled by the fabric of her pajamas.

Kit shushed him. Leave it to Jordan to douse her with gasoline and then accidentally light up a cigarette.

The sound of movement upstairs stopped her in her tracks. No one yelled for help. No sounds of violence or struggle. She wished she could still the rapid beating of her heart. Then again, if she stood here much longer, she might get her wish.

Heavy footsteps on the stairs forced her to act. She dove beneath the kitchen table and waited quietly as the footsteps came closer. What did she honestly think she was going to achieve here?

A pair of brown loafers came into view and she bit her lip to keep herself from crying out. She prayed that Jordan had the good sense to remain silent.

The brown loafers stopped at the sliding glass door. She heard the turn of a lock and then the door slid open. Clearly, the intruder decided to go back outside the easy way. He left the door open, not bothering to close it behind him. Her cheek pressed to the cool tiles of the kitchen floor, Kit watched as the intruder disappeared into the darkness.

"Kit," Jordan called as the sound of a siren drowned out the rest of his statement.

Kit bolted from her position under the table and took the stairs two at a time. She hoped that it was a simple robbery and that Thora had been left unharmed.

She pulled her phone from her waistband. "Jordan, I need to hang up. The police are here and I want to check that Thora is okay." She clicked off the phone and poked her head in the first bedroom. Judging from the lack of clutter, Kit decided that this wasn't the master bedroom and continued down the hallway.

"Thora," she called, her voice cracking slightly. "Are you okay?"

The lack of a response spiked Kit's blood pressure. The next room was empty, too.

"Kit," Romeo's voice boomed. "Kit, are you here?"

"Upstairs," she called. She stood at the base of Thora's bed, looking around the room.

Romeo appeared in the doorway, unkempt and unshaven. "What are you doing in here? Are you hurt?"

Kit hugged herself. "I'm fine. I came to help Thora, but she isn't here." She gestured to the neatly made bed. "She must be sleeping somewhere else tonight. I think we should check with Phyllis."

"Did you get a look at the intruder?" he asked.

She shook her head. "Just his shoes. Brown loafers, a little worn."

"We didn't see anyone outside," Officer Harley said, stepping into view. "He came in through the back window. There's glass everywhere."

Romeo surveyed the room. "Doesn't look like a robbery, does it?" He walked over to the dresser to inspect the jewelry box that sat in plain sight. He opened it to see orderly rows of jewelry that included diamonds, emeralds and pearls.

"The other bedroom was neat as a pin," Kit commented. "Did you check the rest of the house?"

Officer Harley nodded. "They're doing it now."

"I hate to wake up Phyllis," Kit said, "but can we see if she knows where Thora is?"

"Absolutely," Romeo agreed, taking her gently by the elbow and guiding her back downstairs. "Cute slippers, by the way."

Kit glanced down at her feet and wiggled the bunnies. "They were a gift from the crew on my show. Well, these were from the lighting guys. The other guys gave me a bottle of George Clooney's tequila and edible underwear." Her cheeks colored. "Long story."

Romeo eyed her curiously. "I don't think I want to know."

As they crossed the front yard, Romeo stopped to give instructions to Officer Jamison. Kit saw that Phyllis was already awake and standing on her front porch, her hair wrapped in oversized curlers. In fact, most of the neighbors were awake and milling around outside in their robes.

"She's not there," Phyllis called as Kit approached.

Kit sighed inwardly. That was a relief. "Someone broke in."

Phyllis lowered her voice. "Did they take anything?"

"Nothing noticeable." She glanced back toward the house and saw Romeo jogging over to join them.

"No evidence that anything's been taken but we'll need to verify that with Thora," he said.

"Not like she'll remember every piece of crap she owns," Phyllis said, "but by all means, give it a try."

"Where is she?" Kit asked.

"She's spending the weekend at her niece's house," Phyllis told them. "It's another Breckenridge birthday. There are so many of them now, I can hardly keep track."

"Why is her car in the driveway?" Romeo asked.

"Her niece came to pick her up. Thora rarely drives herself anywhere these days, but she doesn't like to admit it."

"Did anyone else know that she'd be away this weekend?" Romeo asked.

Phyllis looked thoughtful. "It wasn't a secret, but it's not like she talks to a lot of people about her personal affairs."

142

"Do you think the intruder knew she was away and came looking for something?" Kit asked Romeo.

Romeo shrugged. "Well, he didn't come looking for jewelry." He fixed his gaze on Phyllis. "Anything else she keeps in the house that might be valuable?"

"She has an antique handgun," an ornery voice said. Adelaide Pye stood at the bottom of the porch steps, leaning on her metal crutches for support.

"Adelaide," Phyllis scolded her.

"The police should know," Adelaide insisted.

"She has a license for it," Phyllis said, shooting Adelaide a scornful look.

"Do you know where she keeps it?" Romeo asked. "We should make sure it's still there."

"In the kitchen drawer," Kit replied and all eyes shifted to her. "I saw it the other day when we had pie."

"You were invited in for pie?" Adelaide exclaimed. "I've lived on this street for more years than I care to remember and I've never once been invited in for pie."

"I can't imagine why," Phyllis muttered.

"Can we focus on the gun, please?" Romeo interjected.

"She moved it under her mattress," Phyllis said.

"When?" Kit asked.

"She listens to you," Phyllis said with a shrug. "Apparently, you said the kitchen drawer wasn't sensible if she was planning to be murdered in her sleep."

Romeo rolled his eyes. "I'll go take a look. Thanks." He hustled down the steps and back across the street to Thora's house.

"First a murder, now a break-in?" Adelaide queried to no one in particular. "I knew this town would go downhill once we started letting outsiders in."

"You're free to move somewhere even more insular," Phyllis pointed out. "I hear Connecticut is nice this time of year."

Adelaide huffed and ambled back to her house, the click of her metal crutches on the concrete echoing in the darkness.

"She should just shut up and let people feel sorry for her," Phyllis murmured.

"Do you have the niece's number?" Kit asked, ignoring the jibe at Adelaide. "We should probably call."

Phyllis waved a dismissive hand. "I'll call her directly. We both have cell phones, you know. We're not relics." She bustled into her house and returned with her phone.

"No, that's just your guns," Kit shot back. "Are you going to text her?"

"I can't text because of my arthritis," Phyllis said. "But sometimes I get Siri to do it for me."

"I'll play the role of Siri," Kit volunteered and Phyllis handed her the phone. She typed a message to Thora and wondered if Thora would even get the message before she returned home.

"Gun was there. Nothing obvious was taken," Romeo said when he came back from Thora's house. "The sooner we speak to Thora, the better."

"Thora said she'll come back tomorrow afternoon," Kit announced, reading the reply text. "She doesn't want to miss the pancake breakfast."

"Glad to see she has her priorities in order," Romeo replied archly.

"You've never had her niece's pancakes," Phyllis retorted.

Romeo touched Kit's arm. "Show's over for now. Do you want me to walk you home?"

She smiled up at him. "I live right there, you know."

"I know."

"And I went into Thora's house knowing there was an intruder inside. I'm not easily intimidated."

"Pretty foolish if you ask me," Phyllis chimed in.

"No one asked you, Phyllis," Kit said.

"Sweet dreams, Kit," Phyllis called over her shoulder as she retreated into her house.

Kit and Romeo walked back across the street and stood on Kit's front lawn.

"Maybe when this is all over, you and I can have a conversation that doesn't revolve around crime." Romeo smiled and Kit noticed the faint dimple in his chin for the first time.

"Where's the fun in that?" she asked, nudging him with her shoulder.

"I'll show you," he said, and then added with a wink, "someday."

Kit listened to her Practical Wisdom professor with half an ear. Although she enjoyed the philosophical musings of stout Professor Grove, her mind was stuck on the previous night's events. She knew she should be more shaken up than she actually felt. She couldn't help it, though. She wanted to understand why someone broke into Thora's house, whether it was connected to Ernie's murder. After all, the story had just gone public and then there was an intruder in the house next door. Could that possibility be a coincidence? Did it mean that geriatric Thora had been involved in Ernie's death? Was she holding on to a piece of evidence that the killer hoped to retrieve?

"Miss Wilder, what would be your response?" Professor Grove inquired, his gaze fixed in her direction.

Kit's deer-in-the-headlights expression didn't go unnoticed.

"Remind us of Socrates' view on phronesis," the professor urged. At least he was friendly about it and not snapping his fingers in her face like one of her directors used to do. It had taken all her strength not to bite him.

"He equated it with virtue," Kit replied, struggling to recall the text that she'd read a few nights ago. It all seemed like a blur now.

"Good. And what is virtue?"

Kit racked her brain. Patience is a virtue? No, that wasn't it. "Goodness?" she squeaked.

Professor Grove slapped his desk in excitement. "Yes. And how do we demonstrate goodness? What does it mean?"

A dozen hands shot up. Clearly, other students had followed the reading more carefully. Kit listened as a young man talked about moral and ethical strength. That good people acted reasonably and intelligently. Kit chewed on this idea for the remainder of the class. Thora struck her as a good person, albeit odd and a little spoiled. Could she have contributed to a murder because she'd acted unreasonably and unintelligently? Then didn't that make her a bad person?

146

"Miss Wilder, you look confused," Professor Grove remarked.

Kit felt the heat rise to her cheeks. "I just feel like there are situations where a person might act unreasonably or unintelligently and still be a good person at her core."

"Aristotle believed in real world applications of this concept," he replied. "He thought that life experience would help a person put their goodness in context, to take other factors into consideration and act accordingly."

Thora certainly had a lot of life experience. Had she taken other factors into account and acted accordingly? Everyone said that Ernie was a jerk of epic proportions. Maybe Thora had decided to threaten him with her Derringer, not intending to shoot him, and things had gone horribly awry. Good intentions, bad outcome. Kit had her own personal list of those. Sadly, these situations happened all the time. That fact didn't stop her from hoping, however, that Ernie's murder was not one of those times.

Kit was pleased when Romeo texted and asked her to meet him at Provincetown Pancakes. At this rate, she'd need to start exercising twice a day. She hadn't remembered Westdale being this fattening. For a brief moment, she wished she had enough money to fly Hans out for a fitness boot camp. Those days were over, though, and she needed to accept it.

Romeo was in the same booth as the last time they'd met here. She tried not to label it as 'their booth.' It was definitely too soon, especially considering their interactions to date all centered around a murder.

"How was class?" he asked. "What was it today, The Art of Quiet Contemplation?"

"That's insulting," she said, sliding into the seat across from him. "It was Practical Wisdom."

He snorted, taking them both by surprise. Kit laughed. "I didn't peg you for a snorter."

"I'm not, usually." He seemed slightly embarrassed in a way that Kit found charming.

The server appeared as if summoned by magic. "Hi Miss Wilder. Will it be a short stack with a side of blueberries today?"

Kit blinked. She remembered her order from last time? "Um, sure."

The server turned to Romeo. "Divine Sampler?"

He nodded crisply, equally in awe.

The server cracked her gum and smiled. "Everybody's got a talent for something." She took their menus and walked back toward the kitchen.

"I think this is my new favorite place," Romeo said. "I've been going to the diner in my neck of the woods since I was a kid and no one there ever remembers what I order."

"Where is your neck of the woods anyway?" Kit asked.

"I grew up in Philly," Romeo said.

"Is that where you live now?"

"No, my folks are there, but I live on the outskirts of Eastdale."

"No wonder you get here so quickly. Do you actually hang out in Fanatics? Is that why you were there?"

"I like a good sports bar as much as the next guy," he replied diplomatically. "But I was there to speak to your boyfriend Delfino."

148

The server returned with two glasses of water. Kit noticed her wink at Romeo as she turned away.

"I guess she's your fan now," Kit observed dryly.

Romeo grinned. "Jealous?"

"It's nearly as bad as losing half my Twitter followers during the last purge."

Romeo cocked his head. "I have no idea what that means, but I'll take your word for it." He opened the cloth napkin and unfolded it neatly onto his lap. "So I've been thinking about the break-in."

"Me, too," Kit exclaimed. "It was distracting during class. Professor Grove could tell I wasn't fully there."

"I don't think this was a random burglary," he continued. "I think it was related to the murder, but I haven't figured out why."

"Did you find out for sure whether anything was stolen?"

"Thora hasn't been able to identify any missing items."

"And you trust her judgment?" Kit queried. "I mean, I like her a lot, but she stored an ancient Derringer in her kitchen drawer between the can opener and the pink polka dot birthday candles."

"Point taken," Romeo said. "Do you think it's odd that she moved the gun to under her mattress after the story broke?"

Kit bit her lip. "Like she hid it because she knew someone might try to take it to prove her involvement?"

Romeo shrugged. "Maybe, although I had a look at the gun. I don't think it could blow an ant off a picnic basket."

"She moved the gun because of me. I made fun of her for storing it there and suggested it be closer to her bed. If

149

an intruder comes at night, she's not going to be sitting around in her kitchen, is she?"

"She is old," Romeo said. "Don't elderly people develop insomnia?"

"Still. Why keep it in her kitchen drawer if she intends to use it to defend herself?"

"She lives in Westdale," Romeo pointed out. "It's the safest town in the Mid-Atlantic. What makes her think she'd have an intruder at all?"

Kit blew out a breath. She had no clue. "Is there a chance that the intruder was looking for me?"

Romeo's chin lifted. "You mean because of the article? Some idiot thought they were breaking into your house?"

Kit nodded. "You said I might get a few stalkers."

Romeo rubbed his temples. "I hadn't considered it, but I guess it's possible."

"What about the motor home or Paul's brother?" she asked. "Any progress there?"

The server appeared and set down their respective plates. Kit thanked her, but the server's eyes were glued to Romeo.

"This looks amazing," Romeo said. "I think there's extra sausage." He looked immensely pleased with this unexpected outcome.

"Enjoy," the server said.

"Thanks." Romeo scanned her uniform for a nametag. "Thank you, Polly."

"No problem. Let me know if you need anything else. Anything at all."

Kit was sure that Polly had added an extra wiggle to her walk for Romeo's benefit. Too bad for her that he was focused on his overflowing plate of food.

"How can you eat all this?" Kit asked. "You clearly have excellent metabolism." She frowned. "I hate men. They're so lucky."

"I don't overdo it on beer. I work out, like you." He hesitated. "Well, probably not like you. I don't Zumba or whatever. I lift weights and box. I'm also over six feet tall."

Kit stabbed her pancakes. "I box, too," she mumbled.

"We haven't been able to track down the motor home or Carl," Romeo told her.

"And do you think that's because they're together?" Kit asked.

"Hard to say. The thing is, we can't locate Paul either."

Kit paused mid-chew. "Paul? My stable guy?"

"I think you'll find he's employed by your mother, not you," Romeo said good-naturedly.

"Did you get his address from Huntley?"

"We did and we spoke to his siblings. They hadn't seen him in days and hadn't seen Carl for over a year."

Kit's mind was racing. "Paul's a good person. I feel it in my bones."

"The way Ernie felt it in his bones?" Romeo queried. "You saw how they ended up."

Kit shook her head adamantly. "Paul is not involved. No way." She tried to drum up an alternate suspect. "What about Peregrine? Can't you make her talk? We could always get perps to talk on Fool's Gold."

"Easy when they have scriptwriters who tell them what to say," Romeo said.

151

"We had consultants," Kit protested. "Real life cops. Guys from covert ops. Lots of people with real world experience to make it more authentic for the audience."

"We're not covert ops," Romeo replied. "And we're not a television show."

Kit bristled. "I think we should take another stab at Peregrine...literally." She held up her fork.

"Now, now," Romeo cautioned. "You don't want to make comments like that to a detective." He pushed his plate toward her. "Sausage? There's plenty."

Kit pushed the plate back toward him. She didn't want his sausage. Not today anyway.

Chapter Nine

Now that Kit was living in her new home, she was finally starting to settle into a routine. She was a creature of habit and felt best when she was organized and in control.

After homework and an hour of cardio, Kit decided to water herself and her front garden, hoping to revive some of the sadder-looking flowers. The fact that the flowers were still alive suggested that one of her neighbors had been secretly tending to them. Kit knew which neighbor she'd put her money on.

As she sprayed the borders on the right, she noticed Myra Beacon knocking on Peregrine's door.

"Her car isn't there," Kit called, stating the obvious.

Myra abandoned her post at the front door and met Kit on the lawn.

"Who knew you had a green thumb?" Myra said.

"I don't know if I'd go that far," Kit replied. "Let's leave it at opposable."

Myra gestured to Peregrine's house. "Have you seen her lately? She hasn't returned my calls."

Kit turned off the hose and dropped it on the ground. She'd been so focused on Thora's house that she hadn't paid much attention to Peregrine's.

"Now that you mention it, I haven't seen her in a few days." She tried to remember the last time she'd seen her neighbor. "Not since right after the break-in at Thora's house."

Myra's hand flew to cover her mouth. "There was a break-in on the street?"

Kit realized that yet another crime was being swept under the carpet for the sake of Westdale's pristine reputation. She'd need to have another word with Crispin.

"Nothing was stolen," Kit reassured her. "And Thora wasn't even home at the time."

"That's odd, isn't it?" Myra said. "That nothing was taken."

"Well, no one's certain," she said. "Thora's not exactly reliable when it comes to remembering things."

Myra chewed her lip. "Do you think we should go in, make sure everything's okay?"

Kit stared at the pretty house. "I don't want to break a window. Peregrine would probably sue me."

Myra produced a key from her handbag. "No breaking and entering required."

Kit didn't love the idea of going into Peregrine's house without permission, but Myra had her worried. What if something happened to Peregrine the way it happened to Ernie? What if the break-in had been a diversion?

"I'll come with you," Kit said.

Together, the two women walked cautiously toward Peregrine's house. Myra used her key to unlock the front door and stepped over the threshold calling Peregrine's name.

"What do you think you're doing?" a voice called.

Kit stopped in her tracks. Adelaide Pye stood on the sidewalk, eyeing them suspiciously. Kit wasn't sure how to respond. She didn't know Adelaide well enough to determine whether to trust her.

"Kit, are you coming?" Myra urged.

Kit watched as Adelaide made her way up the driveway, struggling a little with her metal crutches. She felt a rush of sympathy for the woman. It seemed that Adelaide still wasn't wholly comfortable using them.

"Is she home?" Adelaide asked.

"We're checking," Kit said. "She hasn't replied to Myra's calls and we want to make sure she's okay."

"I'll come, too," Adelaide said, leaving no room for argument. She climbed up the steps and pushed her way past Kit. "Damn, she is a neat freak, isn't she?"

"You haven't been in here before?" Kit inquired. She imagined her elderly neighbors sitting around in each other's houses and lamenting the shortcomings of the next generation.

"Peregrine Monroe, are you stuck under something large and heavy?" Adelaide's loud voice echoed throughout the quiet house. "Knock once for yes."

Stuck under something large and heavy? Kit's thoughts flew to Ernie and his crushed chest. She dashed into the living room, her stomach lurching.

"I don't think she's here," Myra called from upstairs.

The living room was also empty.

"What's going on?" Phyllis appeared behind Kit.

"How'd you get in here so quickly?" Kit asked.

"She rode her scooter across the street," Adelaide said. Then Kit heard her mutter under her breath, "Lazybones."

"You're welcome to get your own scooter," Phyllis told Adelaide. "Then again, you probably get more sympathetic looks with the crutches."

"Phyllis!" Kit scolded her.

Myra joined them in the living room. "You can stop looking. I think she's gone."

"What do you mean 'gone'?" Adelaide asked.

Myra wrung her hands nervously. "Some of her drawers are empty. I think she's flown the coop."

"I'll call Romeo," Kit said, pulling her phone from her pocket and texting him.

"We finally fill one empty house and now we have another," Adelaide huffed. "This street is cursed. Did you know this land belonged to the Lenape Indians before the settlers arrived?"

Phyllis rolled her eyes. "If you feel that strongly about it, then why don't you give your house back to them?"

"You'd love that, wouldn't you?" Adelaide sniped. She pounded one of her crutches into the floor. "I'm not going anywhere until they carry me out in a wooden box."

"That can be arranged," Phyllis replied. "Just ask Ernie. On second thought, you can't."

"Ladies," Kit cautioned them. "Can we focus on the fact that our neighbor has gone AWOL?"

"How about we focus on the fact that Phyllis's sense of decency has gone AWOL?" Adelaide moved to cross her arms indignantly before realizing that she was constrained by the crutches.

"I'm going back to the office," Myra said. "Let me know when we figure out where she is."

Kit's phone pinged and she read Romeo's reply text. "He's on his way."

"Better go fix your hair then," Adelaide said. "Looks unkempt."

Kit's hand flew involuntarily to her head and she smoothed a few wayward strands.

"That's not remotely better," Adelaide said.

Kit had the sudden urge to shove one of those crutches in a painful place. She dismissed the thought, though, knowing that a certain good-looking detective was on the way.

Half an hour later, Kit waited outside while Romeo and his friends combed the premises. Thankfully, Adelaide and Phyllis had returned to their respective homes, restoring peace and quiet to the neighborhood.

"Looks like she took her necessities and then some," Romeo said, dropping down beside her on the front step.

"Do you think she's on the run?" Kit asked. She still couldn't imagine that a woman like Peregrine Monroe was involved in a murder.

"I'm not sure. I'm going to call the police in Sedona and see if she's staying with her sister."

"Do you think she found out that we know about her and Carl's involvement? I wouldn't put it past Chief Riley to feed her information."

"She definitely left for a reason," Romeo agreed.

"It was after the break-in at Thora's," Kit commented. "Do you think it's a coincidence? Maybe we are on the right track. Maybe the break-in is related to Ernie's death."

Romeo patted her thigh. "Do me a favor and stop thinking, at least for a bit."

Kit straightened. "That had a whiff of condescension, Detective Moretti."

Romeo rubbed his forehead. "Kit, I appreciate your help on this, I do. But you're not a real detective or cop or anything remotely related to law enforcement. Need I remind you that this is a murder case. I don't want to see you get hurt."

"I don't want to see you get hurt either," she said, pulling herself to her feet. "So maybe you should stop thinking, too."

Kit stalked across the lawn and jumped with ease over the bushes between the two houses. She retreated inside, slamming the door behind her. She'd endured enough macho crap during her years in Los Angeles. She wasn't willing to put up with it now, especially not on her home turf.

Her phone rang and she saw Francie's face smiling back at her. "Hey there."

"Hi. Charlotte and I are in Butter Beans doing our psychology homework. Do you want to meet us here?"

"I would love to," Kit said. "Be there in ten."

Any excuse to leave the scene of the latest Westdale crime.

Francie waved from a chair by the front window and Kit returned the greeting. It was so nice to feel like she had real friends. Other than Jordan, none of her Hollywood friends made an effort to get in touch now that she was blacklisted.

A few people had even stopped following her on Instagram, although she pretended not to notice.

"I'll grab a drink and be over in a sec," Kit said and went to the counter. There was no line and Sam was behind the counter, pounding away on the keyboard of his laptop.

"Ellie," he cried happily, setting his laptop aside. "What can I get for you?"

"It's Kit, actually."

"I know," he said, grinning, "but you'll always be Ellie Gold to me."

"Well, I'd prefer to be Kit Wilder when I'm in here, if that's okay."

He was nonplussed. "Sure thing. Skinny vanilla latte?"

"Green tea today, Sam."

He rubbed his hands eagerly. "Changing it up. I like it." He set to work, humming the theme tune to Jurassic Park.

"So what are you working on?" Kit asked, gesturing to the laptop.

Sam brightened. "I'm glad you asked. It's a crime thriller about a mute kid and a jaded cop."

"What happened to cowboys in space?"

He shrugged. "Overdone. There's a role for you in this one."

"Oh, really? Am I the jaded cop?"

"No, you're the heroin-addicted girlfriend he's trying to rescue."

"Charming." She forced a smile.

He handed her a steaming mug of tea. "On the house."

"No thanks, I'd like to pay." She pulled money from her wallet and set it on the counter. "See you around, Sam."

159

Francie and Charlotte were deep in conversation when Kit approached.

"So what are you two working on?" Kit asked, sitting down beside Charlotte.

"We were working on Professor Wentworth's assignment, but I just got a text," Francie said, holding up her phone as proof. "Is it true that Peregrine Monroe had Ernie killed and is on the run?"

Kit's eyes popped. "Honestly, who needs the Gazette?"

"No one," Charlotte replied earnestly. "That's why it's hemorrhaging money."

Kit decided to ask Crispin about that the next time she saw him. "Peregrine has left town," Kit explained, "but that's all we know. Romeo thinks she probably went to Sedona. He's checking with the police there."

"Do you think she's responsible?" Francie asked, lowering her voice.

Kit exhaled. "I'm so confused. She's ice cold and has OCD tendencies, but I don't think that makes her a killer."

"Yes, but if she hired a killer, though," Francie said, "wouldn't that make sense? I mean, women like Peregrine Monroe don't do their own laundry, let alone more serious dirty work."

Kit sipped her tea. "You may have a point."

"Who did she hire?" Charlotte asked.

"A guy named Carl. His brother Paul tipped me off. He's our stablehand."

Charlotte's expression brightened. "Oh, that's right. You have a horse. You're so lucky. My father was always afraid to let me ride because of my dyspraxia, but it's actually supposed to be good exercise for me."

"You're more than welcome to ride Peppermint," Kit offered. "I feel guilty that she's not stretching her legs often enough."

"I would love to," Charlotte enthused. "Do you think I could come to Greyabbey one day?"

Charlotte sounded so hopeful that Kit felt guilty for not inviting her sooner. "Absolutely. I'm sorry, I would've asked you sooner, but I've been so wrapped up in the murder investigation and school."

"I understand," Charlotte said.

"She's under a lot of stress," Francie added, nodding to Charlotte. "Between her dad's cancer and her stepmother…"

"Please don't call her that," Charlotte snapped.

"Sorry." Francie's pale cheeks colored. "Anyway, I think horse riding would be a good stress reliever for her."

"You're welcome to come, too," Kit said, aware that Francie and Charlotte were generally inseparable.

"Thanks, I'd love to," Francie said.

"How about tomorrow?" Kit suggested. "Come to my place for lunch and then we'll go over to Greyabbey."

"Lunch in the dead man's house?" Charlotte queried softly.

"It's not the dead man's house," Francie scolded her. "It's Kit's house."

"I know, but still." Charlotte looked apprehensive.

"I'm sure we could have lunch at Greyabbey," Kit relented. In fact, she knew her mother would be thrilled, especially because Francie and Charlotte were deemed appropriate companions for Kit. She didn't want to give her mother the satisfaction of pleasing her, though.

"That would be amazing," Charlotte said. "I've always wanted to see Greyabbey up close. Does your mother really keep lizards in the billiard room?"

"Ugh, I hope not," Kit replied. She hadn't been in the billiard room since her return. She dreaded to think what other surprises were in store for her now that she was home.

Chapter Ten

Kit opted to drive the golf cart to the stable with Francie and Charlotte. With the uneven ground, she didn't want to risk Charlotte tripping and injuring herself before she even reached the stable.

"I'm so excited to ride Peppermint," Charlotte said, clapping her hands.

Kit was happy to be able to do something nice for her friend. All these years Charlotte could have been engaged in an activity that she loved, an activity that would have benefited her. Unfortunately, common sense had taken a backseat to fear in the Tilton household.

"As you know our stablehand has been MIA, so I'll need to get Peppermint saddled up," Kit said. She didn't elaborate, not wanting to implicate Paul any further. She was sure that he was an innocent person caught up in his brother's criminal activities.

"It's so peaceful here," Francie said, admiring their quiet surroundings. "You'd never know how close we are to town."

"Not that Westdale is a buzzing metropolis," Kit remarked.

"Well, the crime statistics sure have shot up since you arrived," Francie teased. "Must be that Los Angeles vibe you give off."

"I do not give off a vibe," Kit objected, bringing the golf cart to a halt beside the paddock.

Peppermint wasn't out in the paddock so Kit went to look for her in the stable. To her surprise and relief, Paul was there, cleaning Peppermint's feet with a hoof pick.

"Paul," Kit greeted him warmly. "I'm so glad to see you." She resisted the urge to hug him in case he took it the wrong way.

Paul lowered his head. "I'm sorry I've been avoiding....well, everyone."

"Have you spoken to the police?" she asked, fairly certain that he hadn't.

"Not yet, but I will. I tried to do some digging on my own first," he said. "I wanted to get some answers."

"Did you get in touch with him?"

Paul bit his lip. "I think maybe he had something to do with it."

Behind her, Charlotte gasped and Paul's cheeks colored in response.

"Carl ain't a bad guy. Whatever happened, I'm sure it was an accident."

"Would you mind if I called Detective Moretti now to come and speak with you?" Kit asked gently. "If you're ready. It just looks bad that you took off." Like Peregrine.

His gaze flickered to Francie and Charlotte. "I think so, but I don't want to mess up your day with your friends."

"Don't mind us," Francie said. "Do what you need to do."

"Paul, this is Francie and Charlotte. They're friends from school."

164

"Nice to meet you," he said. "I'd offer to shake your hands but" — He held up his dirty palms — "you'd probably prefer not to."

"She's such a beautiful horse," Charlotte said. "Can I pet her?"

"She'd love it," Paul told her. "Go on."

As Charlotte eagerly moved toward the horse, her shoulder brushed the stable wall, causing a pitchfork to fall forward. The metal prongs scraped Francie's arm before clattering to the stable floor.

"Ow," Francie cried, gripping her bicep tightly. Kit could see the blood streaming down her friend's arm and dripping onto the floor.

"Omigod, Francie," Charlotte gasped, rushing to Francie's side. "I'm so sorry. It was an accident."

"I know," Francie said weakly. If anyone was accustomed to Charlotte's accidents, it was her best friend.

"Can I take a look?" Paul asked. He waited for Francie to nod her approval before gently removing her fingers.

Francie squeezed her eyes closed as Paul appraised the wound.

"Okay, this ain't exactly a tourniquet situation but we could do with applying direct pressure. Since I don't have a sterile cloth handy..." Without another word, he whipped off his T-shirt and wrapped it once around Francie's arm, pressing firmly to stymie the blood flow.

Kit's mouth dropped open. "Holy cow," she breathed.

"I've never seen anything like it," Charlotte added.

"As much as I wish you were, I know you ain't referencing my First Aid skills," Paul said.

They weren't. They were staring at Paul's bare chest and, sadly, not because of his impressive pecs. It was concave, like someone had pushed a battering ram into his sternum and he lived to tell the tale.

"Paul, I don't mean to be rude, but I need to know," Kit asked, anxiety twisting her insides. "What happened to you?"

To his credit, Paul continued to apply pressure to Francie's wound, not covering himself like he probably wanted to.

"It's a Krasensky curse," he explained. "Runs in the family. We hide it pretty well under clothes, though. That's why you never see me or Carl hanging out in our swim trunks." He grinned in an effort to hide his discomfort.

"That's a genetic condition?" Kit queried, She'd abandoned the trying-not-to-stare position. This was too important.

"Mama said it's called pectoral excavatum. An inward defect of the sternum." He said it slowly as if he'd memorized the description of his condition. "You can get surgery to correct it, but it's too expensive."

"And both you and Carl have this condition?" Kit asked.

"So did my grandaddy. Didn't keep him from attracting the ladies."

Kit pulled out her phone and began to tap the screen.

"What's wrong? Do I need an ambulance?" Francie asked.

"No," Kit said. "We need the police. I know who the murderer is."

By the time Romeo arrived at Greyabbey, everyone was gathered in the garden room with glasses of lemonade, except Heloise who'd added a little extra kick to hers.

Kit greeted him at the door with Huntley hot on her heels. Huntley preferred to be in the thick of things when the opportunity presented itself.

"So this is Greyabbey," Romeo said, leaning casually against the doorjamb. "I can see why you were so anxious to get back to your house. This place is a dump."

"This dump has been featured in Architectural Digest." Heloise appeared in the entry hall, flanked by Hermes and Valentino. Kit thought they'd look like hellhounds protecting the devil if they weren't so darn cute.

"I beg your pardon, Mrs. Wilder," Romeo said, lowering his head.

"Mrs. Winthrop Wilder," she corrected him.

"Yes, ma'am," he said and Kit stifled a laugh. Finally someone else was facing her mother's wrath. Kit decided that she should invite Romeo over more often.

"What's the emergency?" Romeo asked, straightening his suit jacket in an effort to appear professional.

"There's someone here we'd like you to meet," Kit said, gesturing for him to follow.

They returned to the garden room and Romeo took notice of each person in the room, as well as the multiple bird cages.

"Hello ladies," Romeo said, nodding in Francie and Charlotte's direction. He gaze shifted to Paul, who was now sporting a loose black T-shirt thanks to Huntley.

"I'm Paul Krasensky," Paul said.

Romeo shot Kit a quizzical look. "Is this where you've been holed up? With all the rooms in this place, it's no surprise we couldn't find you."

"I take in stray animals," Heloise said, "not people."

"Heaven forbid," Kit whispered.

"What's with the crowd?" Romeo asked. "Unlike you, I don't usually perform for the public."

"Paul has something to show you," Kit said.

Paul began to remove his top. Romeo opened his mouth to object until he saw Paul's concave chest.

"Meatballs and gravy," Romeo whispered. "It's Carl."

Kit lightly touched his arm. "I think it is."

"What's going on?" Heloise demanded. "Are we supposed to be a captivated audience? If so, you need a better hook."

"The body from my house isn't Ernie Ludwig," Kit announced.

"What are you talking about?" Charlotte asked. "Who else could it be?"

Kit's expression softened. "I'm sorry to tell you this, Paul, but I think the body in my house belongs to your brother. I think Carl is dead."

Paul nodded solemnly, as though it was the news he'd been expecting. "I loved him a ton, but Carl was always getting himself into trouble. It was only a matter of time before something like this happened."

"Peregrine had hired Carl to rough up Ernie in the hope of getting him to fix up his house or leave town," Kit explained to a few confused faces.

"But Ernie was already planning to skip town in his motor home because of his mounting debts," Romeo

168

interjected. "Carl must've stumbled upon him at the wrong time."

"Like in the middle of his exit strategy," Kit said. "An exit strategy I think he'd already planned after a visit from Chief Riley, also at Peregrine's request."

"So isn't that what Peregrine wanted?" Francie asked. "Why would Ernie need to kill Carl if he was leaving town?"

Romeo looked thoughtful. "Hopefully Ernie can tell us himself...when we find him."

"So Ernie killed Carl and buried him underneath the floorboards?" Charlotte asked, aghast.

"Then he put down that ugly carpet to cover it up before he left," Kit explained. "That's why there was one room with brand new carpet that didn't match the walls. He didn't care what it looked like. He just needed to hide the evidence for as long as possible."

"Why didn't it smell?" Charlotte asked and then shot a pained look in Paul's direction.

"It probably did at one point," Romeo said, "but the house was closed up for a long time before the foreclosure process began."

"What a horrible man," Francie said with a shiver.

"So is he the one who broke into your neighbor's house?" Charlotte asked.

"I think so," Kit said. "Which means he's probably still lurking nearby."

"Why would he do that?" Huntley asked. "Shouldn't he be hiding in a Third World country by now with an umbrella drink and an assumed identity?"

"That may have been his original plan," Kit said, "until Thora spotted him in Naples, Florida. She'd convinced herself that she'd imagined him."

"And that was easy to believe, knowing Thora Breckenridge," Huntley added.

"But Ernie saw Thora, too," Charlotte said. Her hand flew to cover her mouth when the realization hit her. "He wants to kill her to keep her quiet."

"We need to get officers stationed near the house," Romeo said. "He knows Thora saw him and, thanks to the Westdale Gazette, he knows that we've found the body."

"He's probably been monitoring the website for news ever since I bought the house," Kit explained. "He always knew there was a chance the body would be discovered and now that it has, Thora is a liability."

"Thora spotting him wasn't a problem before?" Francie asked. "Why now?"

"Because everyone thought he'd fled town anyway," Kit explained. "The fact that he was alive would've been no big deal to everyone except for the debt collectors."

"Once the body was found, though, he had a problem," Romeo said. "Initially, he figured that if the body was ever found, the police would assume it was his, but Thora threw a monkey wrench into that plan."

"So where is he now?" Heloise asked.

"He's in hiding, obviously," Kit said. "He can't risk anyone else recognizing him. He's probably staying in a nearby town until he can risk another try at offing Thora."

"He won't wait long," Romeo said. "Each day brings the risk that Thora will tell someone." Romeo stared at Kit. "How good of an actress are you?"

170

Kit's eyes widened, understanding. "Most actresses avoid playing older women, but I'll make an exception for you."

As Kit pulled the short white wig over her pinned up hair, she channeled the Big Bad Wolf dressing up as the grandmother. She disliked casting Ernie in the innocent role of Little Red Riding Hood, but she needed to bring her snarl to the scene. She couldn't do that if she channeled the sweet grandmother.

Thora was staying with Phyllis for the second night in a row. She left during daylight so that there was little chance Ernie would see the bait and switch in action. If he was coming back, no doubt he'd wait until nighttime to strike. Kit hoped tonight was the night. She wanted to get this over with.

Kit's FaceTime app alerted her to an incoming call. "Yes, ladies?"

Thora and Phyllis squeezed their faces into the tiny image on her screen. "We want to see how realistic you look," Thora said. "Your makeup was a little questionable last night. Ooh, nice hair. I think I like it better than mine."

Kit touched the wig. "Thanks."

"Any sign of that bald turd?" Phyllis asked, her usual blunt manner on display.

"Patience, Phyllis," Kit said. "He may not show tonight either."

"But he will show eventually, won't he?" Thora asked and Kit heard the anxiety in her small voice.

"Romeo thinks so," Kit replied. "Time isn't on his side. The sooner he keeps you from talking, the better."

"Oh, well if Romeo thinks so," Phyllis said, exaggerating the detective's name. Thora followed up her friend's statement with kissing noises.

"Maybe I'll just help Ernie find you," Kit threatened and Thora's puckering ceased.

"I haven't seen any police outside," Phyllis remarked. "Are you sure they're here?"

"You're not supposed to be peering out the window," Kit said. "You're supposed to be acting normal."

"That is normal," Phyllis argued. "How do you think I know what goes on around here?"

"Okay Golden Girls, I'm going now." She didn't wait for their protests. She tucked the phone into her back pocket and wandered upstairs to look out the bedroom window. Why didn't Phyllis see any police? Romeo said they'd be there again, just like the night before.

She stood behind the curtain and peered outside. The streetlights were bright and plenty of windows across the street showed signs of life. She'd hate to see Phyllis's electric bill next month. Every light in the house seemed ablaze. Under the circumstances, she doubted that Ernie would come straight down Thornhill Road. More likely he'd return to the back of the house where the yard was bordered by tall trees. Maybe that was where the police were hiding — behind the trees. If it was Harley, though, he was probably up a tree with no idea how to get down. He reminded Kit of a toddler.

Kit debated calling Jordan out of boredom. That was how she'd handled boredom on set when she wasn't in a scene. Of course, Jordan was usually able to join her. Now they were separated by multiple time zones. She missed her friends. She missed her life.

Sighing, she plopped down on the edge of Thora's bed. A romance novel sat on the bedside table. Thora read romance books? She knew Huntley was a fan of the genre, but she wouldn't have pegged Thora for one. Kit picked up the book and examined the bare-chested man on the cover. Not too shabby. He reminded her of a guy from her gym in L.A.

A noise downstairs grabbed her attention and she set down the book. It wasn't as loud as glass shattering, more of a hard clunk.

She climbed under the covers and closed her eyes, feigning sleep. She wanted to look like easy prey so he'd drop his guard. Then the police could swoop in and do their thing.

Creak. Creak. Kit stiffened. Thora should really have those floorboards fixed.

She heard the soft footsteps coming down the hallway. Almost time for her big scene. She kept still and focused on her breathing, just like she did in the episode when Ellie Gold was kidnapped by a serial killer and tossed into the trunk of a car. When the trunk opened later, the serial killer had to think that Ellie was still unconscious. She'd accidentally hit the actor in the face with the gas can in the first take. He'd needed makeup to cover the bruise so they could shoot the scene again. As much as she wanted to laugh at the memory, she was too frightened.

Her bottom began to vibrate and she realized in horror that her phone was in her back pocket. Why hadn't she turned off the phone? As muffled as the sound was, there was no way Ernie didn't hear it.

Sure enough, the footsteps halted. Kit continued to play Sleeping Beauty and prayed that the vibrations would stop. In the dim light, Ernie would only be able to see the top of her white head. She tried to picture him in the doorway without opening her eyes. She hoped he hadn't decided to bring a gun. Romeo had thought it was unlikely and she trusted his judgment.

The phone fell silent and Kit waited for Ernie to make a move. When would the police burst in? They hadn't discussed the logistics. It wasn't like Ernie had to try and kill her. They just needed to apprehend him…and a confession wouldn't hurt.

A breeze passed her cheek and she realized that Ernie was standing beside the bed. Would he be able to see the youthful glow of her skin? Maybe she should've done more to age her face.

Something crashed down onto her face and Kit bit into the fabric. A pillow. Ernie was trying to smother her with a pillow. Poor Thora wouldn't have stood a chance. Kit, however, had experience with pillow smothering.

She dug her nails into Ernie's arm, drawing blood. He cried out and released the pillow long enough for her to get out from under it. Her wig got caught underneath and it fell off as she gasped for air. She scrambled to the other side of the bed and landed on her feet before Ernie had time to process the situation.

"What?" Ernie blinked in confusion. "You're not Thora."

"And you're not dead," Kit shot back.

He narrowed his eyes. "Who are you?" He glanced at the wig on the bed. "Why are you dressed up like her?"

"Come on now, Ernie," Kit chided him. "Surely, you can put two and two together. Or maybe you can't. That would explain your money problems."

It was then that she noticed the knife in his hand. It seemed that Ernie had a backup plan. Where were those cops? As usual, they were slower than a salt-covered snail. With her back to the wall and only a double bed between them, Kit was suddenly aware of the position she'd put herself in.

"Come a little closer so I can get a good look at you," he said.

"I think your line is 'Grandma, what big eyes you have.'"

"It's not your big eyes I'm looking at," he sneered and Kit felt a strong desire to kick him into sterility.

"Drop the knife before the police get here," Kit urged. "And maybe they won't shoot you."

"Why do you look familiar?" Ernie asked, squinting suspiciously at Kit.

"I was on TV," Kit said.

"Wait," Ernie said and broke into a lecherous grin. "You're the girl who bought my house. You found the body."

"That's right and I'm very famous. I have five hundred thousand Instagram followers. If you kill me, it will be a high-profile investigation. It won't be like Carl."

Kit caught the flash of fear in Ernie's expression. "You know about Carl?"

"What happened, Ernie? Did he catch you sneaking off in the middle of the night?"

"It was an accident," Ernie growled. "I thought he was one of Delfino's guys. I was in the motor home, packing to leave, and he came at me from behind."

"And you killed him?"

"I had my knife in my hand," Ernie said, holding up the blade. "I was using it to cut off a piece of duct tape. Carl surprised me and I reacted." He sounded more annoyed than apologetic.

"That's kind of you to bring the murder weapon along," Kit remarked. "It'll save the police some trouble."

Ernie glanced around the dark room. "What police? Why aren't they here to protect you? Killing you will be as easy as killing Carl. Even easier because you're just a girl."

"I'm not just a girl, you misogynistic pig," Kit objected. "I'm Katherine Winthrop Wilder."

"You and all those other Mayflower bitches can go to hell," he barked.

Ernie lunged for her and Kit kicked him in the face, catching his cheek. He recovered quickly and came at her again. This time she blocked him with a front kick that knocked the knife from his fist. Kit watched as it slid under the bed. Hans had taught her that move. The kick was second nature to her — a basic fight move that she'd performed on many Fool's Gold villains. Ernie was tougher than he looked too, though. He stumbled back but managed to remain standing. Without hesitation, he launched himself straight toward her. Kit fell against the wall, whacking the back of her head. By the time she regained her focus, Ernie had retrieved the knife from under the bed. She shook off the impending headache and scrambled to her feet.

Ernie was on her side of the room now, gripping the knife. Kit's gaze flickered to the open bedroom door. Despite the darkness, there was enough moonlight streaming in through the window to allow Kit to see where she needed to go. As fast as she was, she still had obstacles in her way, namely, a double bed and a knife-wielding bald guy.

Suddenly, Kit remembered the gun under Thora's mattress. Was it still there? Thora had a valid license for it so there was no reason for the police to remove it.

"You're not getting out of the room alive," he warned.

Keeping her eyes fixed on Ernie, she dove to the side, rolling across the top of the bed. The bed was more cushioned than she'd expected and she bounced, landing in a heap on the other side. Ernie blocked the doorway before she had time to spring forward.

"Enough acrobatics," he growled.

She crab-walked backward toward the top end of the mattress and reached underneath. Her fingers gripped the cold metal and she pulled the gun from its hiding spot. Although it was smaller than the one she was accustomed to holding as Ellie Gold, Kit felt completely at ease pointing it at the criminal in front of her.

"The saints are made of tough stock, Ernie," she said, moving to a standing position. Her confidence grew with every inch she rose. "You should know that, having lived in Westdale."

The second he laid eyes on the gun, Ernie's demeanor shifted and Kit got the sense that she was in control of the situation.

"What show were you on?" Ernie asked. "It's bugging me." Kit could already see the bruise forming on his cheek from where she'd kicked him.

"Fool's Gold," she replied proudly. "I played a cop. I even had my own catchphrase."

"I got your bling right here," Romeo said and Kit looked over Ernie's shoulder to see a pair of handcuffs glinting in the moonlight.

Kit sat on Phyllis's front porch, sipping a peppermint tea and replaying her adventures with Ernie for the neighbors.

"I can't believe he planned to smother me with my new pillow," Thora said. "It said right on the packaging that it posed no risk to my health."

"I can't believe the police took so long to get here," Phyllis grumbled. "You could've been killed."

"A mix-up in communication according to Romeo," Kit said. "They thought it was only a one-night show."

"I'm sure it was Harley's fault," Phyllis said. "That idiot probably set his alarm for ten a.m. instead of ten p.m."

"So is he courting you yet?" Thora asked.

"Harley?" Kit asked, aghast.

Phyllis clucked her tongue. "Thora, nobody courts anymore. They jump into bed without knowing each other's name half the time." Phyllis noticed Kit's incredulous expression. "Don't give me that look. I have HBO."

Kit didn't want to imagine which racy shows Phyllis watched on premium cable.

"Well, it would be nice to have a handsome policeman on the street," Thora said, "especially since Thornhill Road seems to be a hotbed of criminal activity."

Kit pursed her lips. As sweet as they were, she didn't want to share details of her personal life with her neighbors. Not that Romeo was courting her or jumping into her bed.

"Listen, I think we should throw a party to celebrate Ernie's capture," Thora suggested. "I'll even host it."

"Thora, don't do this to yourself," Phyllis complained. "You take on these projects that you can't handle and then everyone has to scramble at the last minute to help."

Kit looked from Phyllis to Thora. "You two are like sisters. Exactly how long have you been neighbors?"

"Long enough," Phyllis said.

"Over forty years," Thora said.

"You can't remember whether you ate breakfast but you can remember that?" Phyllis asked.

Thora shrugged. "I remember the important things."

"Okay ladies, as fun as this evening has been, I really need my beauty sleep." Kit handed her empty mug to Phyllis. "Thanks for the tea."

"Maybe you should court him," Thora suggested as Kit hopped down to the front lawn.

"She doesn't need to court anybody," Phyllis snapped. "For Pete's sake, she just started a new chapter in her life. Why would she rush into a relationship with someone she barely knows?"

"She's such a pretty girl," Thora replied. "She should flaunt it while she still has it. Beauty doesn't last forever. Look at me, I'm yesterday's cover girl."

"I think you mean last century's cover girl," Phyllis shot back.

Kit continued to her house across the street, the sound of their argument fading. Even though the squabble was about her, her participation didn't seem to be a requirement.

She stepped inside her house and closed the door behind her. Phyllis was right. She was starting a new chapter in her life. Now that she was here, she couldn't wait to see what happened next.

The day of Thora's party arrived and Kit was relieved to see that it was cloudless and warm. That meant they'd stay outside. Part of her didn't want to revisit the inside of Thora's house anytime soon.

Kit carried a tray of brownies to the long table set up in Thora's backyard.

"Did you make these or did you have Diane do it?" Phyllis asked with one skeptical eyebrow raised.

"I made them," Kit insisted. "I even added white chocolate chips. See?" She held up the tray for closer inspection.

"Hmpf," Phyllis said, taking a brownie and biting it in half.

"Phyllis," Kit scolded her. "Those are for dessert."

"When you get to be my age, waiting for dessert could mean you don't get any. Ever."

"Don't be ridiculous," Kit said. "You're not that old." Kit regretted the words as soon as they left her mouth. In actual fact, Phyllis probably was that old. She just hid it better than most.

"Too bad Peregrine won't be joining us," Thora remarked, appearing behind them with a stack of cloth napkins.

"Well, she was lucky the police didn't charge her with anything," Kit said.

"Luck had nothing to do with it," Phyllis scoffed. "Unless luck also goes by the name Chief Riley."

"Or Ted Bingham," Thora said. She glanced at Kit. "Her lawyer."

"Peregrine claims she didn't hire Carl to hurt Ernie," Kit told them. "She only asked Carl to use his influence to persuade Ernie to fix up his house."

"And there's no one left to dispute her version," Thora said knowingly.

"So why did she sneak off?" Phyllis asked. "Did she explain that?"

"Her sister apparently suffered a stroke and she rushed to Sedona," Kit explained. "Romeo verified her story, but he still thinks she snuck off because she thought that Carl killed Ernie and she'd be held responsible. It's likely that the break-in at Thora's scared Peregrine into thinking that Carl would come back to silence her."

"Good riddance to her," Phyllis said. "It isn't just a messy yard that brings down a neighborhood."

"Do we know anything about the people who bought her house?" Kit asked, looking at Phyllis. She seemed to be the direct line to all the Westdale gossip.

"Not yet," Phyllis replied. "But let's hope they're better than the last neighbor who moved in. What a nightmare."

Kit hip checked Phyllis before realizing her mistake. "Oh Phyllis, I'm so sorry," she said. "See, you seem so young that I forget how old you are."

Phyllis rubbed her hip. "Good thing for you this is a replacement."

Thora licked her lips. "Forget the brownies, the real treat just arrived."

Kit followed her gaze to see Romeo striding across the lawn to greet them. Instead of his usual suit, he was dressed in pale blue shorts and a torso skimming black T-shirt. Leather sandals completed the casual look.

"I hope you don't mind that I invited him," Thora whispered. "But tough if you do. This shindig needs eye candy."

Kit went to elbow Thora in the ribs but then thought better of it. She really needed to adjust to her elderly companions. She was used to physical contact with the other actors on set.

"I almost didn't recognize you," Kit teased as Romeo approached them.

"You've seen me in my summer casual clothes before," he reminded her.

"Hiding in a booth in Provincetown Pancakes," she pointed out. "You're out in the open here. In broad daylight no less."

Romeo glanced around at the neighbors, soaking up the party atmosphere. "I guess I am."

He produced a box from behind his back and handed it to Kit.

"What's this?" she asked.

"A token of our appreciation," he said, "for helping us bring Ernie to justice."

She opened the box to reveal an oversized cupcake decorated with a pair of gold handcuffs. "How sweet. Thank you."

"I tried for a bottle of tequila and edible underpants, but the department rejected it." Romeo broke into a broad smile that set Kit's heart alight.

"Cupcakes are an acceptable substitute."

"You'll be pleased to know that Carl's remains finally turned up and the DNA results confirmed that the body is Carl's," Romeo said.

Kit cocked her head. "They turned up?"

"Let me guess," Phyllis interjected. "They mysteriously disappeared until Peregrine was no longer a murder suspect."

"Nothing mysterious about it," Romeo remarked. "Harley and Jamison were the ones who supposedly dropped the remains at the M.E.'s office."

Kit understood. If Chief Riley believed, like Peregrine, that Carl had killed Ernie, then he would've hidden the body to slow down the investigation. Harley and Jamison did as they were told. She'd say one thing for them, Westdale protected its own. Too bad for Carl that he hadn't lived in Westdale.

"Would you mind if I had a private word with Miss Wilder?" Romeo asked the two older women.

"Take all the private time you need," Thora said. "My room's available if you need it. Thanks to Kit, that's the most action my bedroom has seen in a decade."

Kit blushed furiously as Romeo steered her toward quiet corner of the lawn.

"Now that the investigation is over, I thought today might be the day we have a conversation that doesn't revolve around crime," he told her.

"Where's the fun in that?" she teased, echoing her earlier statement. Looking at him now, she had the feeling that the fun was only just beginning.

Thank you for reading A Dead End! I hope you enjoyed the first book in the Saints & Strangers series. If so, please help other readers find this book ~

1. Write a review and post it on sites like Amazon, GoodReads and LibraryThing.
2. Sign up for my newsletter and check out keeleybates.com so you can find out about the next book as soon as it's available.
3. Like my Facebook page.
4. Don't miss The Deep End and The Bitter End, the next books in the series.

Read on for an excerpt from The Deep End ~

The Deep End
Chapter One

Kit Wilder struggled to pay attention to the man lecturing her. To be fair, he was a professor of ethics so lecturing was a major part of his job. To Kit, however, it seemed like he was giving her a stern talking to and she tended to tune out that particular frequency. As her head lolled to the side, she felt a heel slam down on the top of her foot.

"Ouch," she yelled and quickly regretted it. Professor Philbrook's eyes shifted to her.

"Miss Wilder, is there something you'd like to add to the discussion?" he asked.

"Sorry. Leg cramp," she replied and scowled at her alleged friend Francie, the young woman attached to the offending heel.

Francie kept her gaze on the professor, but Kit detected the hint of a smile.

"Perhaps more potassium in your diet then," Professor Philbrook said and resumed his lecture.

Kit did her best to listen attentively for the remainder of the class. It was difficult, though, when the topic was eye-wateringly dull and the professor's voice reminded her of the sound of whales communicating underwater.

She glanced at the empty seat on the other side of Francie, the one where her friend Charlotte usually sat. Kit sighed inwardly; things could be worse. She could be like Charlotte, keeping her sick father company in his final days.

John Tilton suffered from colon cancer and the doctor recently advised the family that the end was near. Charlotte had been missing classes in order to spend as many waking hours as possible with her dad. Kit understood the desire. When she was eighteen, her own father died of a heart attack on the golf course of the Westdale Country Club. It was sudden and there had been no opportunity for goodbyes. Five years later, she still missed him every single day.

Class drew to its merciful end and Kit immediately turned to chastise Francie. "I know you're best friend isn't here for you to torment, but I don't appreciate being used as a substitute."

Francie collected her belongings and tossed them into her Prada shoulder bag. "You need to pay attention in class. I promised Charlotte that we'd take excellent notes for her. That means you and me. We can't allow her to fall behind."

Kit softened. "Fine," she grumbled and followed Francie out of the classroom and down the corridor of Hampshire Hall.

The truth was that Kit was still adjusting to student life after a five-year gap. She'd left the leafy, affluent town of Westdale, Pennsylvania at eighteen, spurred by her father's death. She'd headed to Hollywood, much to her mother's dismay — a feeling that Heloise Winthrop Wilder made abundantly clear when she revoked Kit's trust fund in retaliation.

Luck had sided with Kit. Within weeks of her arrival in Los Angeles, she snagged a leading role on a new television show, Fool's Gold, where she rose to fame as a young detective called Ellie Gold. Four years later she found herself blackballed in Hollywood with a reputation as a diva, a rebel rouser, and an all-around troublemaker. While it was true that she ranted on Twitter about the poor treatment of crew members, was photographed wearing Converse sneakers on the red carpet, and reported a line producer for several instances of sexual harassment, Kit didn't think her actions warranted a permanent dismissal. She wouldn't have done anything differently, though. As far as she was concerned, she'd stood up for people who didn't have the clout to stand up for themselves and stayed true to herself. She couldn't help it. The courage of her conviction was a personality trait she'd inherited from her father and she had no desire to change it.

Kit spent her fifth year trying to worm her way back in through smaller roles, but it wasn't meant to be. She still hoped that she'd be welcome back in Hollywood at some point, but her chain-smoking agent, Beatrice Coleman, warned her to be patient. Wait for the memories to fade or for the producers responsible to fall out of favor. In the meantime, Kit was biding her time in her hometown of Westdale, home of more Mayflower Pilgrim descendants than you could shake a rainstick at. She'd reluctantly agreed to do what her mother had wanted five years ago — she'd enrolled in college. Westdale College was prestigious and private and it didn't hurt that the college was within her mother's sphere of influence. Heloise Winthrop Wilder was legendary in Westdale, a fact that Kit was reminded of every day now that she was back in the fold.

"We should call Charlotte and see how she's doing," Francie suggested, once they'd reached the outer doors.

They stepped into the gray haze and Kit felt a raindrop dissolve on her cheek.

"Can we do it from inside Butter Beans?" Kit asked. "I'm not exactly the Tin Man, but I don't want to get wet."

Francie rolled her eyes, tossing her blond ponytail to one side. "You spent too long in L.A., Kit. We need to toughen you up again. Get you back to your Pilgrim roots."

Kit blanched. "If by 'toughen up,' you mean 'conceal, don't feel,' you should be aware that it's the Winthrop family motto." Kit gave her an earnest look. "I'm serious. It's on the crest and everything. Anyway, I already have a mother trying unsuccessfully to shape and mold me. I don't need another one."

"You're preaching to the choir," Francie said, holding up her hands in a defensive gesture. Like Heloise, Cecelia Musgrove was a pillar of the community with an interest in maintaining certain, illusory standards.

The two young women dashed across Standish Street in an effort to reach the door of the coffee shop before the deluge began. As the door clicked closed behind them, the heavens opened and a torrent of rain swept down the street, banging angrily against the windows.

"A narrow escape," Francie said.

Kit arched an eyebrow. "Is there any other kind?"

In the elegant study of a five-bedroom country estate, Rebecca and Charlotte Tilton waited. A pot of tea and half-eaten sandwiches covered a small, round table. Rebecca, the elder of the two sisters, sat patiently in their father's leather chair while Charlotte, red-cheeked and wild-eyed, paced behind her.

"This is ridiculous," Charlotte seethed. "We should be in there with him. She may act like a child, but we're his daughters."

Rebecca responded in her usual temperate manner. "And Jasmine is his wife. She has every right to be in there with him."

Charlotte scoffed. "She's been his wife for half a minute. It doesn't count. We both know she doesn't love him."

"But he loves her," Rebecca said, her voice soft. "And what does it matter now?"

The door swung open and Dr. Farrell entered the study, followed by Adele, the round-faced hospice nurse who'd been assisting Rebecca in caring for her father in his final weeks. The two sisters rushed over, their expressions hopeful. Wordlessly, the doctor shook his head. Rebecca sighed deeply while Charlotte promptly burst into tears.

"Thank you for everything, Dr. Farrell," Rebecca said, shaking his hand. "I know Father appreciated all that you did for him."

"Don't thank me. Not many women would put such a promising medical career on hold to care for an ailing father." He gently patted her arm. "John Tilton was a good man. I wish I could have done more."

"Such a sweet man," Adele added. "It was an honor to get to know him these last couple of weeks."

"Thank you, Adele," Rebecca said to the nurse. "You've been an incredible help to us all."

"You girls take good care of yourselves," Adele said. "Your father loved you very much, you know. He wouldn't want you to mope for long. Chin up. That's what he says, isn't it?"

"It is," Charlotte acknowledged, offering Adele a grateful smile as the nurse left the room.

Dr. Farrell gave each girl a sympathetic kiss on the cheek. "Someone from Landau's is on their way to collect him. Be sure to send me details of the party."

Rebecca nodded. Her father had insisted on a party at Oak Lodge, their family home, rather than a tearful funeral service. "He's right to want us to celebrate his life. It was a good one."

As Dr. Farrell slipped out the door, Rebecca placed a comforting arm around her sister's shoulders. "Would you like to see him one more time before they take him away? Jasmine's probably gone by now."

"Already off to max out his credit cards, no doubt," Charlotte muttered.

"Charlotte, try to keep a civil tongue," Rebecca chastised her. "I'm sure Jasmine's grieving in her own way."

"You seem to confuse grieving with celebrating a windfall."

Rebecca shot her a warning look before they stepped into the darkened room. Even though their father could no longer hear them, Rebecca wanted to remain respectful of his second wife.

After a last, quiet moment with their father, two men arrived from Landau's to remove John Tilton from his home. It was bittersweet for Charlotte. Although she was relieved that he was no longer in pain, she hated to part from him.

Charlotte and Rebecca retired to the living room where they stared listlessly at the television screen. Charlotte didn't recognize the show but she didn't care. Her father was gone. Her mother was long gone. She and Rebecca were all alone now.

"We should call the Westdale Gazette," Rebecca said. "Crispin said they'd already drafted a special obituary." Crispin Winthrop was Kit's cousin and the owner and editor of the Westdale Gazette.

Charlotte nodded mutely. The click clack of sharp heels drew her attention to the adjoining foyer.

Jasmine Tilton, a former professional cheerleader before her profitable marriage to John, stood in the entryway. "What time do we expect that creepy lawyer?"

"You can at least pretend to be upset," Charlotte said, her gaze still fixed on the television screen.

Jasmine placed a hand on her hip. "Why be upset, honey? He lived a very full life and now he's about to pass his very full bank account on to his deserving wife."

Rebecca smiled politely. She highly doubted that her father would leave his entire fortune to his trophy wife. As susceptible as he was to a pretty face and an ample bosom, John Tilton was devoted to his daughters.

"Well," Rebecca said, "it is nice to follow tradition and actually read the will before counting your diamonds."

Jasmine examined her coral-colored nails. "No need to read it. I was there when he wrote it. Hell, I practically wrote it for him."

"No doubt," Charlotte said.

The doorbell rang and Jasmine's sculpted eyebrows shot up. "And there's your Daddy's lawyer now."

53829988R00110

Made in the USA
San Bernardino, CA
29 September 2017